Dear

MW01100496

The School
on the Hill

With Compliments

J. Thoadi.

Dec 22 / 2018

The School on the Hill

Ganesh Nadar

Vitasta
Let Knowledge Spread

Published by
Renu Kaul Verma for
Vitasta Publishing Pvt Ltd
2/15, Ansari Road, Daryaganj
New Delhi - 110 002
info@vitastapublishing.com

ISBN 9789386473059
© Ganesh Nadar, 2017

The views and opinions expressed in this book are the author's own.
He is solely responsible for the facts and authenticity of the quotes and
sources used for this work. The publisher in no way is liable for the same.

Cover and layout by Vits Press
Printed by Vikas Computer and Printers, New Delhi

Foreword

So long ago...yet many memories remain.

Memories of daily breathtaking sunrises, except during the monsoon season! Beautiful varied landscapes; with many acres of land and numerous secret places to roam and to play, hide and explore. Award winning views of open fields, bushes, green meadows, long and glittering streams and rivers; with at least twice a day, a never-ending goods train winding around the corner, looking like a shiny and well-fed worm.

All views encapsulated by the distant towering silvery grey hills. To most of us, and especially to the homesick boarders, Barnes was our stone fortress, our safe refuge, our home away from home, for months together, where the air was clean, the curriculum vast and varied, and the food was simple but still plentiful. We worked and played hard, which naturally meant we were in a perpetual state of starvation, wonderfully supplemented by the many fruit trees and bushes on the vast estate, such as figs, mulberries, blackberries, boras, and of course the huge mango trees, with their glossy dark leaves and fruit so plentiful that we could usually gather our fill from the windfall on the ground, hardly ever needing to pluck them from the branches above. If we were still hungry, there were the tuck shops; two most favourite haunts, stuffed with seemingly magical and incredible edibles.

Barnes was by no means perfect. Like every institution, it had its dark side; numerous and severe punishments; and teachers who were both bullies and seemingly racists, with faults that would simply not be tolerated today. But that was another world in relatively more tolerant times, but there were wonderful times too.

Long walks to the cinema; after breakfast, weekend market trips; lots of dances during the year in Evans Hall, beautifully decorated by students; Parents Days; School and class plays; midnight feasts; and athletic and gymnastic competitions that lasted for days and were attended by favourite and popular ex-students...and of course – the *Bada Khana*.

Friends and classmates from years ago are still friends.

Yes...many memories linger...of the dear school on the hill.

—*Margaret Andrews* (now *Margaret Pearl*)

Acknowledgements

The first person I must thank is Nikhil Lakshman who told me that I could write. I would also like to thank my publisher Renu Kaul Verma and Papri Sri Raman for forcing me to write the last 10,000 words of this book, I thought I had written enough.

"You have to give the reader value for money so please write" said Renu and I wrote. Am also glad that it came out well. I would also like to thank my editor Bill Koul whose first words were, "This is like an ocean of words, there is no para, no sections, no chapters, was he running while writing"? But! The finished version was amazing. Not a word was cut but they were compartmentalized so well, it was like being in a Japaneese company.

Dear Bill you must know that I left school in 1974. Recalling events after four decades was hazy. Sometimes an event would flash before my eyes and I used to rush to write it before it faded. So I did not have the time to think of paragraphs.

I would also like to thank two friends, Archana Masih and Uttam Ghosh. After they read my first book they told me, "We could hear your voice while reading, it was like you were sitting next to us and telling us the story". Its words like these that make a writer want to write more.

ONE

Barnes (1926-1968)

by W R Coles*

*When afar and asunder, parted are
those who are singing today.*

THESE WORDS from the school song of Harrow,
Sir Winston Churchill's old school, come to mind as I
write of Barnes from 1926 to 1968, the nearly 43 years
I lived and worked there. Truly, my companions and
the children of my early years are all parted afar and
asunder. Yet, like St Luke, it seems good to me, having
followed all things closely for some time past, to write
an orderly account that new generations may know the
truth concerning things.

Barnes - before 1926

Just about 100 years ago, people began to think

---

* W R Coles was second and the longest serving Headmaster

that education for their children should be provided by Government. Before that, there were schools mainly for the rich. For the poor, there were very few schools and those were mostly provided by the Church and charitable people. In the early 1700s, many such schools were established in England. So it was that when the Rev Richard Cobbe was appointed Chaplain to the Honourable East India Company's factory at Bombay that he founded in 1718, in a building not far from the present Cathedral of St Thomas in the Fort, a small free school where 12 poor boys were housed, clothed, fed and educated by just one school master. That Charity School was the grain of mustard seed from which the mighty tree of Barnes had sprung.

A hundred years passed by before another East India Company Chaplain, the Venerable Archdeacon George Barnes, realised that the Charity School could not possibly meet the needs of the hundreds of children at that time without any education. So he appealed for funds and started the Bombay Education Society (BES) in 1815, the oldest Society in the city interested in the welfare and upbringing of children. To start with, a small school was taken over. Numbers grew rapidly until it was apparent that new school grounds and buildings were essential. A large airy site at Byculla was given by Government for the construction of the school. This time, the girl students were also provided for. New school buildings were opened to students in 1825.

One of the copper plates commemorating the opening is now displayed on the wall of Evans Hall, Devlali. The other copper plate remains with Christ Church School, Byculla, which, with the parish church, stands on part of the land given originally to the BES school. Much of the land was later sold to help build Barnes. A photograph of the old school building used to hang on a wall in my office at Devlali. I hope it is still there. When I arrived in India in September 1926, I spent a night in one of the Byculla school buildings. The buildings have long since been demolished to make room for modern blocks of flats.

The BES schools, as they were popularly known in the past, were primarily boarding schools for Anglo-Indian boys and girls, mainly belonging to the Anglican Church. However, day-scholars were also later admitted, from all castes and creeds. For another hundred years, there seems to have been little change. Then in the early 1930s, the BES amalgamated with the Indo-British Institution, which had been founded by the Rev George Candy, circa 1837. Byculla was by then crowded and unhealthy. Plans, initiated by Sir Reginald Spence and Mr Haig-Brown, to move the boarding part of the schools away from Bombay (now Mumbai) to the cooler and healthier Deccan Plateau began to take shape. More than 250 acres of land were purchased at Devlali for the boarding wing.

On 17 November 1923, Sir George Lloyd laid the foundation stone of Evans Hall. Less than two years later, on

29 January 1925, a special train brought the first boarders to Devlali. With old time ceremony, in the presence of many distinguished guests, Barnes was declared open by Sir Leslie Wilson, then the Governor of Bombay and the patron of the BES.

Barnes – 1926 to 1968

This short historical sketch explains much of the present Barnes. It is still primarily, and I hope it always will be, as long as there is need, a place where the poor Anglo-Indian children of the Anglican and Protestant Churches can be given a good upbringing and sound education. It is still a Church school where Christian ideals are practiced and imparted. It is a boarding school, the largest in Western India. It has a long and proud record of service to the community that goes back in time to almost 300 years years or so. More has been added over the years and more still will be added in the future but the school will not, I am sure, belie its history.

The memory of founders and benefactors is preserved in the names of the buildings: Barnes, Candy, Spence, Haig-Brown, and Lloyd. Other names are also remembered, such as Greaves House is named after Sir John Greaves, a prominent Bombay businessman, the founder of a firm called Greaves Cotton. He was the Director of the BES from 1930 and the Chairman of its Managing Committee from 1939 to 1949.

Royal House commemorates Harry Royal, an old boy

of the BES school from circa 1900 to 1910, who became an important officer of the Bombay Chamber of Commerce and Honorary Treasurer of the BES for many years. Other old students may be honoured in a similar way in time to come.

Tom Evans

One name is yet to come and, to me, the greatest of them all, the Rev Thomas Evans, familiarly but not irreverently, known as Tom Evans or just Tom. After being the Headmaster at the old schools at Byculla, since 1910, he became the first Headmaster of Barnes. Without Tom, Barnes would probably not have survived its early years. His portrait hangs on a wall in Evans Hall, which we named in his memory when he retired in 1934. I remember Tom as a short, around five feet two or three inches tall, plump, round-faced man, with a merry twinkle in his blue eyes and a determined chin. That twinkle could change in an instant to a steely blue stare that few could outface. The chin seemed to jut out further at that time. It would be hard to find a more determined and dedicated man than Tom. He moved to Devlali in 1925. While architects planned, committees discussed, and contractors built, it was one man, Tom, a resolute, little man, apparently tireless, who really brought Barnes into being. He controlled, checked, and at times drove around his school staff and the students, servants, workmen and the members of the Managing Committee till it was all complete.

In 1932, Tom became a priest. His attitude mellowed down and he became more embracing, though still, at times, the schoolmaster in him broke through. In his fifties at this time, he was as active as many young men half his age. He was extremely hard to beat at tennis; he climbed the surrounding hills, including Broken Tooth and Kalsubai. On his return to England, he served as a country parish priest for nearly 30 years. He died on 16 April 1962. Truly, it could be said of him, as of St Paul, 'he' had fought a good fight and run a straight race.

Barnes in 1926

The buildings were the same as they are now but only that they looked new, raw and bare in 1926. There were no gardens at that time. The few trees were small and far apart.

There were two separate and distinct schools, one for boys and one for girls, and no one was allowed to forget that. A boy who looked at a girl was in danger of severe punishment. There were separate classes for both genders. In Standard 9th, the top class (equivalent to Standard 11th today), there were four boys sitting for the Senior Cambridge and perhaps two girls. The student numbers in other classes, especially the girls' classes, were small. There were about 250 boarders in all and only a dozen day scholars.

No Indian languages were taught at the school. The boy students learnt Latin and the girl students French. Not much in the way of Sciences was taught and there was no division into Arts and Sciences in the top classes. Besides the Senior Cambridge in Standard 9th, there was the Junior Cambridge in Standard 8th and the Preliminary in Standard 6th. All the boarders were Anglo-Indian or European. Among the day-scholars, perhaps, there were half a dozen Indian children.

The boy students wore white shirts and blue shorts as they do now; but instead of shoes, they wore ammunition (Ammo) boots, the type used in the army. These boots weren't very comfortable but were good for playing football. In the athletic sports, most students ran in bare feet. The girl students wore a blue frock as much below the knees as now above. What they wore underneath is quite unbelievable; they wore knickers and bodices, long stockings, at least two petticoats besides other garments for the colder weather. Above all, for both boys and girls, and staff, toupees were compulsory. It was a punishable offence to be seen outdoors without one. Everyone was firmly convinced, doctors included, that sunstroke lurked for bare heads in the sun.

It was possible to feed children on less than 10 rupees a month. Prices were low for everything and salaries were small too. Our servants earned about 10 or 12 rupees per month compared with nearly 90 rupees per day that they get paid today.

In the school hospital, children were often ill with malaria. That, with toupees and other things, is almost unknown now.

The children's dining hall was upstairs in the big hall. The food was brought upstairs from the kitchens by hand lift.

Similar to the present times, boys and girls never seemed to be contented with their meals and would find fault either with the quality or the quantity of food. So in the 1920s, young people had similar complaints as they have now and it will continue to be like that till the end of time. At lunch time, the staff had their meal on the stage facing the children. For dinner, a very formal occasion, students were expected to wear evening clothes: dinner jackets and stiff shirts for the men and long frocks for the ladies. There was a special staff dining-room where the juniors had to take turns in sitting at the high table with the Headmaster and his wife – a seemingly terrifying ordeal at first.

Most of the games played then were same as they are played now, but without badminton, volleyball or baseball; instead there was some tennis. Unlike today, there was no swimming-pool at that time; just a stream, which had no water when it was most wanted in the hot weather. Yet there was as much laughter and happiness then as it is now, but perhaps not so much studying then as it is now.

The Army Cadet Training – 1927 to 1947

As extension of the Auxiliary Force India (AFI) and the Great Indian Peninsula Railway Regiment (GIP Rly Rgt), the Cadet Company of Barnes School had a strength of two officers and 60 cadets. The Officer Commanding was Lt A A Anthony and Lt W R Coles was the Officer Second-in-Command. Although it may sound a little rigmarole but it was a very real part of life at the school from 1927 to 1947. All the senior boys had to join as cadets as soon as they turned 15.

The cadets wore regular army uniform: khaki shorts and tunic, grey shirts (everyone called them grey-backs), 'Ammo' boots and everlasting putties that had to be continually wound and unwound and rolled up tightly. And, of course, extra-large army toupees, with the GIP flash. As accessories, there were webbing belts and shoulder straps, ammunition pouches, haversacks and knapsacks; real bayonets and rifles. They seemed to weigh a ton to the new recruits. The armoury was in the steel-doored room next to the science laboratory and the clothing store was in the room leading off the present Standard 10th Science classroom. Parades were held on Friday evenings and Saturday mornings - before breakfast. There was endless polishing of boots, belts and buckles. Thank goodness, the buttons and badges were black.

Company - Attention! Slope - Arms! Present - Arms! Punctilious smartness was drilled into every cadet before a ceremonial parade; and no amateur stuff was tolerated. A regular Staff Sergeant from the army put the Company through its paces; every cadet chucked out his chest at the Guards of Honour for Lord Brabourne, Sir Roger Lumley and others. Boots were useful for their click when smart turns to right or left were ordered, but their weight on route marches, with resulting blisters, caused such pain!

Highlights of the year were the shooting classification and the annual camp with the rest of the battalion. On the 25 yards miniature .22 range in the school, the early training was done. Then came the annual classifications into 1st, 2nd and 3rd class shots. This was done with live .303 ammunition on the military ranges. The kick of the recoil bruised many a shoulder. The butts party, whose duty was to look after the targets and signal back the scores, took more delight at waving the red flag for a miss than at planting the white disc over the bull.

We did not live under canvas in camp every year but we nearly always joined in on the big field day, the final parade and all the sporting events. One of the darkest secrets in the history of Devlali remains how, one year, Devlali was captured by the Barnes Cadets. Boxing night saw at least half a dozen Cadets matched against the privates and corporals of the other companies of the Regiment.

With the coming of the war (WWII), in 1939, those AFI certificates gained in school became very valuable. The victory in WWII, in 1945, was closely followed by India's independence in 1947.

On the very morning of 15 August 1947, all AFI units were disbanded forthwith by an express telegram. So passed a phase of Barnes that will not return!

The 1930s

The 1930s were times of stringency and change. I was married while on furlough in England. The first news we heard on our arrival at Barnes was of a money crisis. All over the world, there was a depression. Trade was bad everywhere. Businessmen went bankrupt. Many people lost their jobs and those who kept theirs had their salaries reduced.

Barnes was affected like everyone else. Apart from the general world-wide trouble, the school had for the first six years at Devlali not paid its way. Every year there were deficits running in tens of thousands of rupees. Because of that, we still owed the builders more than 6 lakh rupees, and every year there was interest to be paid amounting to over 40,000 rupees So, a hard period of austerity had ushered in.

Many of the original staff left around these years. Mr Evans decided to retire in 1934 and I succeeded him as Headmaster in May 1934. I was only 30 at that time and not very experienced. Ahead stretched years of the strictest economy but, gradually, we cleared our debts and learned to live within our means. By 1939, we were beginning to build up the reserve funds. In 1937, we started the Employees Provident Fund.

It was in the early thirties that our first Indian boarders were admitted. We dropped Latin and French. For a time, we taught Urdu; then Hindustani, as preached by Mahatma Gandhi. Lastly, we settled for Hindi. To start with, neither majority of the parents nor the children took kindly to Indian languages. Eventually, we were reconciled to one language and, in addition to Hindi, we had to introduce Marathi too. We did feel that we were badly dealt with.

The winds of change were blowing. Common sense too dictated that we should be reoriented.

With the change in languages, came education about Indian history, emphasis on India on the whole and Asia in geography. For nature studies, about the birds and the beasts, the trees and flowers of India took the place of robin red-breasts, oaks and daffodils.

Co-education became complete in these years, partly as a matter of financial expediency but fundamentally as a matter of principle. The kindergarten classes had always been mixed. Now we added an extra class yearly till all our classes had boys and girls.

My own family was growing up. Rosemary, born in 1932, began attending school. James, born three years later, suffered from dysentery when he was only a few months old and never properly got rid of the germ. In 1935, my wife and I, with the children, enjoyed a six months' furlough in England. Those were the days of Hitler and the Nazis in Germany. Storm clouds of war were gathering thick and fast. In India, the struggle for Independence grew fiercer year by year.

World War II & Devlali

At first, it seemed the war would pass by Devlali but it was not long before changes came. Overnight, part of our school compound was requisitioned and all the land to the west, where we used to have our cross-country runs, around Surprise Hill, was put out of bounds to form part of the new School of Artillery, with its ranges stretching to Square Top and beyond. From a small peacetime garrison of two or three hundred, Devlali and the surrounding area eventually became an enormous Transit Camp, holding at its maximum 70,000 men. They came from Australia and New Zealand, only to be quickly on their way again to the deserts of North Africa. Regiments came from England to go always further east to Burma or Malaya.

Amongst these men and elsewhere, Barnes was well represented, as more and more old students joined the Forces, mainly the Army, though also the Air Force and the Navy. Older girls became nurses or joined as Women's Auxiliary Corps (WAC). Younger men on the teaching staff went off to enlist in the Forces. Gradually, it became more and more difficult to find teachers. Retired men and, in some cases, misfits had to be engaged as teachers. At times, classes had to be combined, since no teachers were available at all. While the roll of old students in the Forces grew, from time to time, the sad news of casualties, prisoners of war and deaths on active service arrived. The Military Hospital expanded fivefold to deal with the mounting toll of wounded men sent back from the fighting areas.

Towards the end of 1941, and at the beginning of 1942, war came close to India with the capture of Burma by the Japanese. Of the civilians from Rangoon and other Burmese towns, who managed to escape by air or ship or by trekking over the mountains, some came to Barnes - children and adults both. Three teachers and some matrons joined us in this way.

At one time, it seemed there was nothing to stop the Japanese coming into Assam, Bengal or even further. For a period, they had command over the sea. It was considered possible that planes from an aircraft carrier might bomb Bombay and Devlali. So at Barnes, we set to dig trenches, erect blast walls, learn First Aid and undergo training in Air Raid Precaution (ARP). At any hour of the day or night, the Headmaster could be seen, and heard, cycling around the compound, blowing on a whistle. At the first shrill blast, everything had to be stopped, even a meal, and all had to troop off to their Air Raid Stations. Thank goodness, this phase did not last long.

Every effort was made to entertain the troops. We had some wonderful cricket matches against teams that included top club players from Australia, and football games with teams that included one or two professionals from the English Leagues. Individual soldiers were invited to our homes. Most of them appreciated a little touch of home; just to sit quietly and relax, have a cup of tea and a chat, mostly about their families.

Professional artistes from the stage and screen, organised by a special Government Department, ENSA, were sent around the big troop centres. In Devlali, at first, all the entertainments were held in Evans Hall. We took in most of the Chapel and all the balconies. Even then, so great was the rush that even Colonels did not mind sitting on the floor in the aisles. In those days, Barnes saw a variety of shows, orchestras, and plays of all and every kind. What is now the School of Artillery Children's School, near the Cathay Cinema, was built as the Lumley Canteen. One night a week, till the canteen finally closed down at the end of 1947, a team of the staff of Barnes used to run it, first preparing food, and then serving it. By the end of it, all we could do was to cut bread, prepare sandwiches, and pour tea with the rest. In a two-hour period one night, we served 968 cups of tea, which works out about eight cups a minute.

Feeding the boarders during the war was not easy. We used to get our milk from the Military Farm, but at just a week's notice, we had to make our own arrangements. Potatoes, which in pre-war times came from Italy or East Africa, were often nonexistent. If it was not wheat, it was rice, or sugar or something else, which could not be had for love or money. Luckily, it never happened that there was a shortage of everything at the same time.

Our class-work suffered inevitably from lack of proper staff and also from the booming of guns practising on the ranges throughout day and night. Such handicaps were also experienced in England with the air raids. The Cambridge School Certificate examining body let up a little on their normal standards. Our children had to write their answers in pencil, with carbon copies, so that if the ship carrying one set of answers was sunk, there was the second set which might get through in with safety. One year, the question papers did not arrive in time. Unluckily for the candidates who hoped to be excused from taking the examination, fresh single papers were flown over and the printing was done in India.

Destruction and death touched Barnes. The disastrous dock fire and explosion in Bombay brought orphans to the school. Their fathers had been killed while on duty with the Fire Brigade. In 1944, tragedy struck the School itself. Three boys were killed by the explosion of a mortar shell, which they had found just outside the school boundary and were investigating those shells at the rear of Candy Block.

Despite distractions and disasters, life went on. In 1941,

Mr and Mrs Fernandes were married and the wedding
reception was held in Evans Hall. Mr Fernandes worked
for the BES from 1918 to 1924 at Byculla and from 1925
onwards at Barnes until he retired in 1965. He was in-
charge of the school office and the Headmaster's secretary.
Mrs Fernandes was a teacher from 1937 to 1964. Between
them, they served the school for well over 70 years, which
must surely be a record for any school. My son, James, had
another serious attack of dysentery in 1942. It was decided
my wife should take him and Rosemary home to England.
Their journey by sea in the midst of the war was perilous
even though their ship went round the Cape of Good Hope
and almost into the Antarctic to keep clear of submarines.
In England, they went bang into the air raids of the Battle
of Britain. At last, D-Day[1] came, followed by victory for
the Allied Forces in Europe. A year later, after the atomic
blasts at Hiroshima and Nagasaki, the war in Asia too came
to an end.

The Partition

The din of the war ceased but the turmoil and struggle
for independence in India went on, to be brought to a sad
climax with the Partition. The separation of East and West
Pakistan caused much bloodshed and a gigantic refugee
problem. Formerly, there were few Sikh and Sindhi children
in the school. Now they came in dozens and twenties.

More than ever before, Barnes became cosmopolitan in outlook, and was indeed, as all similar schools have been, an oasis where caste, creed, colour or nationalities were of no importance. This was eloquently illustrated on the day Mahatma Gandhi was assassinated. At first, it was not evident who his assailant was and the minority communities in Devlali and elsewhere were fearful. Barnes that night became a haven of refuge for children and adults.

Devlali was now a Transit Camp in reverse. The men who had two, three or four years ago passed through, on their way east, now returned on their homeward way to the west. With them, went families who had lived in India all their lives, whose children had come to Barnes and other such schools. There was fear, of the future and what would be the place of Anglo-Indians in the new India. Our schools were poorer with this exodus, which even now has not ceased. It seemed as if the cream of our teachers and students had deserted us. Yet, if anything, there was better opportunity for employment than before.

Financial aid from Government for schools was continued. Special grants to Anglo-Indian schools were to be cut but only gradually, over a ten-year period. In all this uncertainty, the Managing Committee of the BES debated the advisability of continuing to run Barnes. Long and fierce grew the arguments for and against. Finally, those who thought it wise to close and sell lost. They promptly washed their hands of the Society. On those, whose faith made them vote for continuance, now rested the onus of proving their decision right.

How much they struggled, Barnes today gives evidence.

The Post-Independence Period Struggles

After six months' furlough in 1951, I had barely been back a week before I was asked to go to Poona to look after St Mary's Training College for men and women teachers. The previous Principal had left; the new one was expected to join in a month or two. After handing over the running of Barnes to my First Assistant, I went to Poona. As Barnes, with other Schools, expected its main supply of young teachers from St Mary's Training College, it was a sound policy to keep the college going. As it happened, I had to stay a whole year before the new Principal could come.

Back at Barnes, at the commencement of 1953, life was running once again at its peacetime, at normal pace. Student numbers increased, double divisions were required in some classes. Our studies improved. More children took the Cambridge examination and more passed. The old Junior Cambridge was discontinued. As a war memorial, we wished to build a separate Chapel. In the architect's plans, a school chapel held a prominent place but there was never enough money in the school funds to build one. Since 1925,

---

[1] 6 June 1944

we had been raising our own fund. By 1939, we had about 6,000 rupees As a result of our new efforts in 1946, and the following years, we added nearly another 20,000 rupees. The money was invested with the BES and must have been by now about 35,000 rupees.

The year 1950 was our Silver Jubilee year. Special commemoration bronze medals were struck and awarded to all with any claim to distinction. There were fun fairs, a grand Jubilee Ball in Evans Hall, special prizes, including silver fountain pens. Those of the staff who were celebrating their personal jubilees were given silver plaques or, in the case of servants, Government Saving Certificates.

First Student Right Case

The year 1954 saw another crisis. Mr Morarji Desai in the Bombay Government passed orders that only children whose mother tongue was English could be admitted to Anglo-Indian schools where the medium of instruction was English by constitutional right. All other children were to be compelled to attend Indian language schools whether their parents wished that or not. If persisted, the order meant starving our schools of three-quarters of their students. Ruin, no less, faced us. Mr Frank Anthony, believing that constitutional rights of parents were being invaded, decided, on behalf of all Anglo-Indian schools throughout the country, to challenge the order in the courts. A specific school and specific parents had to be found in whose name the case could go forward. It was Barnes that supplied both. Mr Justice Chagla in the Bombay High Court ruled that the Order was unconstitutional. The Government went in with appeal to the Supreme Court at Delhi. There the Chagla decision was upheld. Our schools were saved and the right of parents to send their children to any school of their unfettered choice was vindicated. Some who had been fearful of opposing Government foretold a difficult time ahead for being the spearhead of the attack. In fact, there was not the vestige of harassment or ill-feeling on the part of the Education Department. On the contrary, our relations with Government became more cordial.

In 1955, 1 became the President of the Association of Heads of Anglo-Indian Schools. At the annual conference that year in Bombay, Mr Hitendra Desai, as Education Minister in the undivided Bombay State, opened the proceedings and made appreciative reference to the work of our schools.

The years 1955 to 1960 were largely a time of preparation. In 1960, all Government financial aid was to cease by our own choice. We could still be eligible for aid but there would be too many strings attached to grants after that. Something over 70,000 rupees a year would have to be made up. Most of it was done relatively painlessly. Our fees from the beginning had been all-inclusive of books, clothing, stationery and so on. Now we asked parents themselves to equip their children with a little more each year. Some small increase in fees was there; but for those entitled to help from the BES resources, there was no cutting back of the provision made for them.

Introduction of the Indian School Certificate Examination

The old Senior Cambridge Examination changed its name to the Indian School Certificate Examination (ISCE) but the papers were still set and marked in England. Only the administration was transferred to India, to be the responsibility, as it still is, of Mr A E T Barrow, the Secretary of the Council.

Mr Barrow taught at Barnes from 1938 to 1944. Later on, in 1966, when he needed an assistant secretary in New Delhi, he took Mr W R King, also on the staff of Barnes from 1950 to 1965.

The year 1963 was to usher in new requirements for passing the ISCE, particularly in Mathematics and Sciences. In the Arts, there was to be little change. Instead of teaching the combined subject called 'Physics with Chemistry', we had to prepare for separate Physics, separate Chemistry and Advanced Mathematics. Since then, we have added, in 1967, another separate subject, called Biology, for the benefit of especially the would-be doctors. Mathematics is perpetually undergoing great changes. The traditional methods of teaching and even the content of the subject are under constant review. It is inevitable in the new, atomic, computerised, modern world.

Figures for year 1958 afford a comparison with those ten years later. In 1958, there were 338 boarders while in 1968 there were over 450. In 1958, 15 girls and boys sat for the Senior Cambridge, of which 14 passed, three in the First Division. In comparison, in 1968, 40 out of 41 passed, with 11 in the First Division. The day-scholar population also fluctuated. In 1958, it was 200, the same as it is today but in-between it climbed to over 250.

The opening of new schools and the expansion of others quite naturally affected our numbers. Some parents whose children had a long way to come to Barnes - an hour's journey morning and evening, preferred schools closer at hand.

Long distance Excursions

The year 1958 saw the first of a series of long distance excursions organised by the school, to places such as Ellora and Ajanta, Mysore, Ootacamund and Bangalore; and Kashmir. The war with China, in 1962, put a stop to those exciting travels. Next, when we tried in 1963, the Railways were so overcrowded that we gave up the idea of further journeys in large numbers. To the south of the school, in the Sayadries, there stands up a 4,500 ft. peak whose correct name is Awandhe, but which for Barnes has always been Broken Tooth. Several times in my early years, I and others had climbed to the base of the Tooth itself without ever getting to the summit. A party of seniors got to the top in 1959 with the help of an experienced climber and ropes, plus local knowledge from the nearby villagers. Soon afterwards, with the arrival of Rev E Goodman to be the school chaplain, a regular outward bound club came into being. Looking back, this period was one of many-sided activities. The School Magazine, which started a new lease of life in 1956 under the title, *The Barnicle*, a short form of Barnes Chronicle, is evidence of this fresh zest.

Duck's Pond Swimming Pool

The early sixties saw the reshaping and enlarging of the old Duck's Pond into a swimming pool to be really proud of. Out of the 170 foot length, often muddy for half the year and more empty during the dry weather, was made a safe and shallow pool for the smallest children; and a senior pool, 25 m long and 4.5 ft. deep, for serious swimming and racing. At the downstream end, a ten-foot deep pool was excavated exclusively for diving, with 1 m, 2 m and 3 m boards. The rough, unkempt, banks of the Duck's Pond were terraced and planted with trees and flower beds. To feed the pool, a well was dug on the northern side and an electric pump installed, so that there would always be fresh water.

Finally, we built dressing-rooms. All this cost something like 40,000 rupees We collected 20,000 rupees ourselves and the BES put in the rest. The new pool was opened in 1962 by Mr N Ferguson, the Chairman of the School Managing Committee.

New School Facilities

Along with swimming pool, three other amenities sprang up in this period - the School Shop, the Library and the senior boys' recreation room. What used to be originally the boys' bathing room at the west end of Evans Hall, though not used for many years, was converted into the School Shop, incorporating the separate and smaller tuck shops for boys and girls, which had so devotedly been managed by members of the staff. Not only the food but also other things from exercise books to football boots, were now always available. A school library had always been in existence but it was only under the Rev E Goodman, a trained librarian before being ordained, that it was fittingly housed, arranged and catalogued. The British Council helped with a magnificent gift of 5,000 rupees worth of new books. Similarly, there had always been recreation rooms for the children but it was Mr MacInnis who showed what could really be made of them, by his development of the senior boys' room.

The equivalent of two classrooms on the ground floor of Spence Block formed the shell. Gradually, by the boys' own efforts, chairs, tables, couches, a radio, record player, games and magazines were added. The whole area was kept spotless and as polished as a new pin.

Barnes' Contribution to the PM's Defence Fund

On the outbreak of hostilities with the Chinese, in 1962, and again with Pakistan, in 1965, Barnes, in company with the rest of India, contributed to the Prime Minister's Defence Fund, made food parcels and provided comforts for the troops on the northern borders and the wounded, some of whom were sent to the Military Hospital in Devlali.

Significant Work before Retirement

In 1963, we passed the 600 mark in our total number of students. My wife, who had been in England with our children since 1942, returned to India in 1964. The next year we went on furlough, contacting Besians wherever we went. That means everyone with connections with the BES schools, such as the old Byculla school, Christ Church, and Barnes. In 1951, while in England, I had the idea of bringing together all three groups in one association. In England, there is an annual get-together. That is where I met most of the Besians in 1965.

On the return flight, we stopped off at Bahrain and were royally entertained by the Kanoos, Jhangianis, and particularly by Malcolm Wrightman and his wife, both one-time teachers at Barnes. In India, the work of Besian, not very active now but that they were active then, is evidenced by the annual Besian Prizes awarded to the best scholars in the top classes. Other Besians are living in Canada, Australia, New Zealand, South and East Africa and in the Persian Gulf; in fact, everywhere.

The plane from Bahrain that brought us back to India touched down safely at Santa-Cruz airport. On reporting my arrival, the Chairman, Mr P S Whaley, asked about my future plans. I pointed out that I was already far beyond the official retiring age of 58 and that beyond the age of 65 years, the Education Department would not permit my further service. It was agreed that I should retire at the end of 1968.

A generous upgrading of staff salaries, with corresponding increases in pay for all grades of workers came into force from April 1966. Concurrently, both boarding and tuition fees were raised. The annual budget hit between 5 and 6 lakh rupees compared with my first, in 1934, of under one lakh rupees. Many of the buildings were reroofed at a cost of half a lakh rupees. It was becoming clearer that a major overhaul of the electric wiring and of the sanitary fittings throughout the school would soon have to be undertaken. From January 1967, a Bursar was appointed to control the business side of the school. I was asked to prepare a scheme for extending the accommodation to take 200 more boarders, aimed to bring the maximum school roll to 600.

Without a much more copious supply of water, that was not feasible in my opinion. Instead, a less ambitious plan was adopted to take the number up to 480. This meant increasing the size of the dining-hall, rearranging the kitchen and storerooms. Each of the 16 dormitories, originally planned very lavishly to hold 25 boarders, at present quite comfortably accommodated 30 boarders. Bathrooms attached to the dormitories were furnished with more showers, wash-basins and commodes. Two other innovations pleased everyone, especially my wife, for she had been telling me for a long time they were really necessary. At the end of 1967, in addition to the old school bus, then 14 years old, a new Standard Herald car was bought. Just before the monsoon of 1968, all the school roads were tar-macadamised. So the months that slipped by consumed with planning for a new era. Our studies improved, culminating in the record success of the ICSE classes of 1968. Our numbers grew; the school discipline was steady and the general tone was as good as it had ever been. More and more money was spent on feeding the boarders. The cost per head per month, which was less than ten rupees in the past, was now 80 rupees. At my last prize giving, I claimed I was handing over the school in a good condition to Mr J L Davis, the incoming Head. I still feel I was justified in my claim.

Post Retirement

I have not gone into complete retirement. At the request of Bishop Luther, I am now the administrative in-charge of Auto-Skills, Nasik, where automobile mechanics are trained. The job is similar to the one at Barnes, but vastly scaled down; 20 students instead of 650, a total staff of ten instead of 60 and more, two or three letters a day to answer instead of dozens; and no parents to interview. As I sit back with less to do and reread this tale of mine of Barnes over the past 43 years, it seems most of my time was taken up in administration and matters impersonal, figures, time-tables, budgets and so on. Of course, that was not really so. There was the staff, teaching, domestic and the more humble bearers, hamals, coolies, who worked with me and without whom nothing could have been achieved. Some stayed a short while only but there were always the stalwarts, with many years of service to give stability and the fruits of their experience. Above all else, were the children for whom Barnes exists and around whom the staff, the planning and everything revolves. Five generations of them have passed through my hands and the wonder still holds me.

Awkward cubs they were when first they came to school. Then they grew in stature, strong they grew in mind till came the time for parting when onward they would go as men to face the world! God be with them all till we meet again.

Onward Barnes

Hear our loyal anthem, as we make it rise

To our School, with all our might;

Barnes has reared us, taught us all the good we prize.

Here we've learned what's true and right.

Chorus:

Onward Barnes! Upward Barnes!

Shall be our watchword and our aim.

Till the echoes ring, let us sing

To your honour, praise and fame.

Awkward cubs we were when first we came to School,

Often grimy, spoilt and slack.

Heavy was the way till we had learnt the rule,

Learnt to know and keep the track.

Grown we are in stature, strong we are of mind.

Now we see they nobly live,

That forsake vain glory, gentle are and kind,

Ever strive their best to give.

Comes the time for parting. Onward we must go.

Face the world as men at length.

But we will remember all the School we owe.

May she grow from strength to strength.

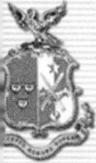

Barnes

The School on the Hill

Devlali.India

Annual Sports Day 196

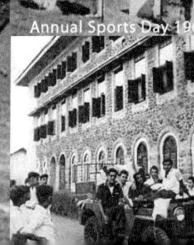

TWO

The Sixth Standard (1969)

Barnes-after Mr Coles

MR COLES left Barnes in 1968. I, Ganesh Nadar, joined the school as a student in 1969. I cannot write like Mr Coles but I'll try my best to continue the story till 1974 when I passed out. Later students can carry on the story.

Ganapathi's First Day at Barnes

The one-horse carriage did not slow down, as it passed the Gate Lodge, which is the entrance of Barnes School at the bottom of the Hill. The horse looked up at the steep incline and started galloping faster. He had ascended this Hill

---

* Photographs used here are contributed by Barnes students over the years and found in Creative Commons spaces

many times in the past with many more people than now.

There was a young boy with his uncle and the tonga wallah who knew his horse would go up easily. The horse went up the Hill with practiced ease, with no help from its master who was busy chewing paan. The horse came to a halt outside the Principal's office, again without bidding. The couple entered the office; the boy looked nervous and the man curious. They met a man sitting at a desk that said *"Bursar"*. The boy, Ganapathi, wondered what the hell did the word bursar mean, but he held his peace. They were ushered into the school Principal's office.

The school Principal, Mr J L Davis, was a tall imposing man, with a gentle smile. He looked at the new student with amusement. With oiled hair and shoes shining, the dark complexioned boy looked very serious for his age. They were told to go to Candy block. The tonga wallah knew the block, as he knew everything else about Barnes. Candy block turned out to be the block furthest from the office. On the way, they had passed Haig Brown, for the girls; Lloyd block, for the kids; Evans Hall, where the mess was; and Spence block which was for the seniors.

They were greeted by Mr D V Hoffman, who was the housemaster there. He was gentle and kind, and had a melodious voice. *"Nadir you go up to the first floor, Keenan come here and help this new boy"* he shouted. Keenan, who was playing hockey at that time, came immediately. The uncle was told that he could not go up to the dormitory and he should now leave.

The uncle, K K Nair, told his nephew, *"Don't worry, I will be back next Sunday"*. Then he left in the tonga. Ganapathi kept staring at the tonga till the horse and carriage disappeared around Lloyd block. Then he followed Keenan upstairs. Keenan helped him carry his iron box and also his haversack. Mrs Banks was the matron for Spence house and she was also new. Later, Ganapathi would find out that even the Principal was new to the school and that he had joined that year only.

It was 9 January 1969 and the new boys were coming in. Barnes had about 10% orphan students who had stayed back even during the long winter vacation. Keenan was one of them. He told Ganapathi to change into khakis and come down with his hockey stick. He was gone before Ganapathi could even reply.

Mrs Banks told him that he should call her Mum Banks and that she had come from England, as the winter was too cold there. Then she counted his shirts, shorts, socks and all his clothes. She taught him how to make his bed. She told him to change when the bell rang for lunch. *"Never mind, you can change later. Go have lunch with those boys downstairs, just follow them"*, she instructed and was gone before he could react. He went down to see his fellow boarders running away from him. They were running towards Evans Hall where the mess was. He walked towards the hall. There were about 30 boys standing in eight different lines. He stood in the Spence junior line which had only three boys.

There was a Master on Duty (MOD), Mr Gama, who was also the sports teacher. He led them in. Lunch was bread, dal, fried fish, and a banana. One of the senior boys said grace and the rest said, *"Amen"*. Ganapathi noticed that there were very small boys in Lloyd block and also a few girls who were giggling all the time. He ate as much as he could. He was choking, as he felt like crying but did not. Owen Keenan, who had helped him up the stairs, told him, *"Eat properly, there is nothing till 3.30 pm"*. It was noon at that time. He ate another piece of bread dipped in dal, which was bland.

After lunch, they were allowed to play till 2.30 pm. Most of the boys were playing hockey. Reluctantly, with Owen urging him on, Ganapathi went up to the dormitory, changed into khakis with other kids and came down with a hockey stick. He joined the game but refused to run, just hitting the ball if it came to him. *"This is not cricket"*, the other boys chided him. But no one scolded him, as he was a new boy.

Another new boy who came the next day was Kishore Thadani, also in Spence house. The two new boys hit it off immediately. It helped that they were both from Bombay. That boy was in the 5th standard; Ganapathi Nadar was in the 6th standard.

On 12 January 1969, the rest of the boarders turned up after their holidays. They were a loud and boisterous lot and treated the new comers as if they were fools. And if any new comer acted smart, he would be ragged to tears. But there was no violence, all tom foolery only.

One of the most difficult adjustments that the new boys had to make was bathing. The old students all bathed naked which made the new crowd nervous. It would take a month before they too joined in. Now they kept their underwear on though the old boarders teased them about it.

Ganapathi's First Day at School

Thirteen January 1969 was the first day of the school. After breakfast at 8 am, there was a short break. Four ST buses came up the Hill and day-scholars came on them. These were special trips only for Barnes students. Many were from Devlali, some from the army and air force camps and a few from Nasik in the distance. One bus came from Devlali, another from South Devlali and the other two from Nasik.

Then there was assembly. Even the day-scholars were in specific houses and they joined their respective lines. The new students asked about their houses and got into their specific lines. Assembly was on the first floor in Evans Hall, above the dining hall, which was on the ground floor.

Barnes occupied an entire Hill. On top of the Hill, there were five big building, all constructed with black stones.

There were no brick buildings. Four of these buildings had four dormitories spread over two floors, each to house 30 students. The class rooms were on the ground floor. The fifth building had a hall on the ground floor, which was the dining area and a hall on the first floor, which had innumerable uses, such as the assembly, examination, gym, and dance; and was also used for exhibitions. On one end, there was a stage, which was used for plays, debates and elocution. At the other end, there was a church, which was used by both the Catholics and the Protestants.

The school Tuck shop was on one side of the building and the biology lab at the other end. There was also a small post office, with its own pin code. Barnes had its own pin code. Then there was this block that was simply called '5'. It had class rooms, a library and the Chemistry lab. There were individual bungalows - for the hospital, for the Principal's office cum residence, for the Vice-Principal's residence and bungalows for various teachers. In the dormitory blocks, at the centre, lived a few teachers. Near Gate Lodge were quarters for the servants who worked there.

At the bottom of the Hill, there was a field for athletics that was also used for playing cricket, hockey and football, depending on the season. There were also three swimming pools; one for the beginners, one for the experienced swimmers and the last one was for diving, with three boards at one, two and three metre levels.

Assembly was at 8.45 am. The students lined up according to their house and marched up in single file, watched by the head boy, Dilip Rao, and the MOD, Mr Gupta, who was also a Hindi teacher. All the teachers were up front. The girls were on one side and the boys on the other. Hymn books were distributed for the new students. The old students knew the hymns by heart. *"Oh God our help in ages past"* was the first hymn they sang. As it was the first day of school, they also sang the Barnes anthem, *"Hear our loyal anthem as we make it rise to the school with all our might, Barnes has reared us taught us all the good..."*

Then the Principal spoke. He welcomed the new students and also the new staff. They had a new Vice-Principal, Mr Roberts, who looked like one of the Kennedys. The Principal also announced the games for that evening, which were hockey for two houses, swimming for one and boxing for the other house. The teachers were the first to leave, followed by the girls and then small boys. Finally, the older boys left, watched by the Principal. The Principal was the last one to leave, with the MOD.

The 6th Standard class was in block '5'. Ganapathi walked towards it, with his books and stationery in his hand. Once he found the class room, he was amazed to hear the noise in it. Students were greeting each other, as they were meeting after a month and a half. Girls sat in the front and boys at the back of the class. The new students waited for the older ones to choose their seats first and then sat down in the remaining seats.

The chairs and desk were attached. There was a latch on the desk, which you could lock. Most students carried a lock with them.

The class teacher, Mr Michael, walked in. He was a grey haired man whose erect bearing was a sight to appreciate. The class stood silently. Then they wished him, *"Good morning, Sir"*. *"Good morning, there is no need to shout, sit quietly,"* he said. The students sat down with a lot of shuffling. Mr Michael took attendance first and then started questioning the new students first. He liked to introduce the new students to the older ones and went out of his way to make them feel at home. He was their English teacher, as well as their Class Teacher.

The bell rang and the next teacher came in. Classes ended at 11.55 am and lunch was served at noon. The afternoon classes began at 1.00 pm and ended at 3.30 pm. The boys rushed to their dormitory, took off their blue and white uniform, and then donned khakis. The black leather shoes gave way to white keds. The blue stockings were replaced by white socks. In 15 minutes, they stood outside Evans Hall for tea, which was a bun, banana and a cup of tasteless tea.

Till 5 pm, it was free games session. Most boys played hockey, some played with marbles and a few chatted about the movies they had seen during the recent holidays. The

MOD kept a watch all the while to make sure none of them sneaked off to smoke.

In the distance, some of the boys could be seen walking near the quarries, which were the source of massive stones that had been used to build the mighty school buildings. These boys were the seniors who had hidden their cigarettes in this area, under rocks. Out came the cigarettes and they shared one cigarette amongst three students. It was just macho bravado; however, they actually did not smoke much. They saw the auto that brought the Tuck shop man into the school. Boys who had some spare money rushed to meet him as, from 5 pm to 6 pm, the shop was out of bounds.

At 5 pm, the bell rang and attendance was taken to make sure no one had run away. These roll calls happened regularly and yet some boys would manage to run away. The roll calls made sure their absence was noticed within a certain time. The boys were usually caught at the railway station.

Spence house had boxing today. Their house captain was also the school head boy, Dilip Rao. First he made them jog at one place and then they went on a run. They went past the quarries, behind Candy block, to the cactus wall that surrounded the school. They went out of the school boundary, where there was a gap in the green wall. They turned left towards Gate Lodge and ran at a gentle pace. At Gate Lodge they turned into the school. Now it became difficult, as they had to run uphill. Some started walking, as Dilip shouted at them. They were soon back at the Gym, which was the other half of the hall where they had their study period in the morning and evening. It was a huge shed, made of tin. Some of the boys skipped, others punched the cement sack that hung there, to harden their hands. A few students could be seen boxing.

Ganapathi wore boxing gloves for the first time in his life. Mr Gama taught him how to guard oneself. He showed him a classic stance where you guard your body with your left hand while the right hand is ready to punch. Ganapathi threw some punches at the teacher who first defended and then attacked his young ward, being careful not to hurt him. He did not want to discourage Ganapathi on day one.

Early Days at School

Classes soon set into a pattern and the games followed. The hockey practice matches were over and now the real matches between various houses started. Boys wore their house colours. A victory earned 2 points, draw 1 and loss 0. As each house had four teams, you could win a maximum of 8 points in a day. There were 4 houses and everybody played everyone else.

Royal house was first, followed by Candy, then Greaves and finally Spence. The boxing matches started next. Boxers were up against others weighing the same weight. This went on for weeks together in the Gym. Only the finals would be held opposite Evans Hall, where a temporary boxing ring would be set up.

The boxing finals were held in the evening, under lights. The judges were Barnes teachers but the referee was from the nearby Artillery camp. It was boisterous. There was a roar of laughter when Christopher Lal came on to fight, as the announcer said *"Lal–Red"* and the students yelled *"CORRECT"!* The winners won gold medals and the losers won silver. Again, the house champions were Royal.

Ganapathi had royalty too among his classmates. There was Masood Alam Khan, whose father was the Nawab of Bela, a Principality in Gujarat. He had a habit of talking about his air conditioned cars and soon the boys were teasing him about his air conditioned bullock cart. He took it all in good spirits. He was a serious kind of boy with impeccable manners and when he spoke in Hindi you knew he was a royalty. Apart from that, he was not good at games nor in his studies. He was very tall for his age but a little sloppy.

Ganapathi's Emotional Reunion with Father

It was a Saturday and Ganapathi was anxiously looking at the road. He was expecting Nair Mama and soon the familiar horse carriage, or tonga as it's known, came pounding past Lloyd block. He was smiling and ran to it. He was taken aback as he was expecting Nair Mama but there were other men in the tonga. His strict father, G Athimuthu Nadar alighted from the tonga, adjusting his white dhoti. Nair Mama was in his customary khakhi pants and a white shirt.

His father smiled at him and asked, *"How are you? Do you like the school?"* *"Yes! I do"*, said the young boy.

Athimuthu Nadar felt tears in his eyes but did not cry. He was very happy to know that his only son was happy in the school. It had broken his heart to send him to boarding school, as he had thought his son had become such a ruffian after his mother's death that no one could control him at home. Nair Mama handed him his customary goodies and then went looking for Mr Hoffman. Ganapathi went into a long speech and tried to tell his father everything about the school in one breath. Athimuthu was perhaps not listening; he was just happy to see his son so involved in his new school.

Mr Hoffman (Hoffy) came out and met his father. *"Don't worry about him, we take good care and he is a very good boy"* he said. Athimuthu Nadar was surprised. In his last school at Bombay, the Principal had complained innumerable times that his son was incorrigible and totally wanton.

He told Nair Mama, *"It was the best idea to send him here"*.

"I told you so" said Nair Mama who was an ex-Navy man and thought nothing was wrong with a boarding school. He had been away from his family for years out at sea and had come out of it none the worse. He still had a clerical job at the Navy in Mumbai.

Soon it was time to part but not before Athimuthu gave Ganapathi a 100 rupees note. Nair Mama was very angry. *"Sir, you will spoil him. His pocket money is 2 rupees a week, and extra pocket money is 4 rupees a week, and you are now giving him 100 rupees. What the hell is wrong with you?"* Mama kept yelling but Athimuthu Nadar kept happily smiling. He could not believe his son had indeed turned into a good boy; he thought he could give him everything that he wanted.

Ganapathi kept waving till the tonga disappeared and then ran to store his tuck with the matron. He handed over the 100 rupees note to Mr Hoffman, who would keep it with his extra pocket money to be withdrawn only on Saturdays. Hoffy would not give him more than 15 rupees at a time. The money was going to last a long time.

The Routine School Life and Homesickness

Mr Henderson was the 6th standard Mathematics teacher. He had a habit of throwing a duster at students who talked among themselves. This caused serious injuries sometimes but that did not bother him. Ganapathi was his favourite, as he was good in Mathematics. Rosemary was very weak in Mathematics; she used to ask Ganapathi to help her and, thus, they became friends. She had a twin sister, Roselin, who looked exactly like her and was in section 6 B.

Nair Mama came to visit Ganapathi every Sunday for

the first month and then made it once a fortnight and finally once a month. One day, Ganapathi got the surprise of his life. He was waiting for Nair Mama and when he came he had brought his younger sister, Saroja, with him. Ganapathi was very happy to see her, as he was very fond of his younger sister. All his other three sisters were older than him. They talked about Bombay and his friends there. When they left, he was sad to see them go. Other parents came and took their kids for the weekend, but Nair Mama always made sure he was back in Bombay the same night.

There was another student, Jimmy Parvaresh, who had a twin, Sharukh, in the 7th standard, because Jimmy had failed the previous year. Both sets of twins were very good in games but poor in studies.

After having tea, the students could do what they wanted till 5 pm. Kishore and Ganapathi spent this hour together usually at the flag post and sometimes under the berry trees. They discussed Bombay continuously. Both were homesick and still had not got used to the boarding life. In the dormitory, they occupied beds side by side and comforted each other when they could not sleep.

While Ganapathi was very good in studies, Kishore was not. Both of them were not good at games. So when there was selection for hockey or boxing teams, they were the last ones to be taken. Both of them lost their first bouts in boxing and were not selected for the hockey teams even though each house had four teams. *"They are choosing old boys, we will be chosen next year"*, they thought as they consoled themselves.

It was a Sunday and Ganapathi was waiting for Nair Mama, who always brought a lot of chocolates and biscuits. He was happy to see Mama had come with his father, Athimuthu Nadar, who was pleased to see his son looking happy. He had thought his son would be homesick, but apparently he had made friends and was perhaps happy in the school. Ganapathi got an additional 50 rupees of extra pocket money on that day. Nair Mama always gave him 15 rupees but his father had given him 50 rupees. He was very happy. His friend Kishore too was happy, as Ganapathi shared his tuck and money with him.

The Examination Day

Soon the examinations were on them. The good students were happy and the slackers were scared. Boys were studying late in the night in the toilets, as you could not keep the lights on in the dormitory.

For the examinations, they had to carry their desks to Evans Hall. Ganapathi carried his own first and then came back to help Rosemary carry hers. Their desks were interspersed with desks of students from other classes - from 6th to 9th standard. The 10th and 11th standard students took the examinations in their own classes.

While he was carrying Rosemary's desk, he was accosted

by the prettiest girl in the school, Jennifer Dameron, who was in 9th standard.

"Are you carrying Debra's desk?" she asked him. Debra was his classmate and Jennifer's younger sister. He blushed and said no. *"Don't you have a girlfriend?"* was her next question. Two other girls walking with her started laughing on seeing his nervousness.

"I don't have any girlfriend and this is Rosemary's desk", he told her.

"Oh, so she is your girlfriend!" she concluded.

"No!" he said, as he was alarmed and ran for his life. The girls started laughing loudly. Jennifer was fond of this dark complexioned and serious looking boy.

Debra had told her that he was very good at studies and behaved very well with the girls.

By the time the desks were all assembled in Evans Hall, the bell rang and the students went to their dormitories. Today was the last day of classes and the next day examinations would start. Games were still compulsory even when the examinations were on. That was the way of Barnes.

Ganapathi was sitting and waiting for the question paper to be distributed. He had written his name and roll number neatly at the top right hand side of the answer paper after drawing the margin with a ruler and pencil.

One of the students in 7th standard called out to him. This was Clyde Arnold, whose elder brother, Glenn, was the

Royal house captain. Ganapathi wondered what this boxer wanted with him. Clyde was pointing towards one direction. He was surprised to see Jennifer smiling at him. *"Best of luck"* she mouthed silently. He blushed and said thanks. He did not wish her back. He was too nervous, wondering why the most beautiful girl in the school was talking to him. Clyde Arnold, seeing him blush, started laughing loudly till a teacher gave him a dirty look.

The paper was distributed and the students started writing with a lot of shuffling around. The good students finished on time and checked their answers. The poorer students kept on writing till the bell rang and, in some cases, the teachers had to literally grab the answer book forcefully from them as the time was up.

First School Holidays – April 1969

On 27 April 1969, after the examinations were over, it was time to go home. Kishore and Ganapathi were so excited they could hardly sleep the previous night. At 11 am, Nair Mama came in a car and Ganapathi was on his way home after saying goodbye to Mr Hoffman, who he was very fond of by now.

Devlali station was full of Barnes boys, shouting at each other and complaining that the canteen at the station was useless. *"We will get what we want at Igatpuri, just wait"* said one to another.

Ganapathi was very happy and surprised to see his entire family in the car. It was an Impalla car and they fitted in easily. He asked his sisters, *"You did not write in your last letter that you all were coming here."*

"We did not know till yesterday, only last night daddy told us that we are going to Shirdi to the Sai Baba temple. Then he told us that we are picking you up on the way", they said.

All his sisters, Dhanalakshmi, Janaki, Vijaya and Saroja had come to receive him, accompanied by their father and Nair Mama. His father's business friend, Manilal, was also with them. It was a jolly good trip, full of noise and laughter. They reached Shirdi in a short while, as it is close to Nasik. At Shirdi, they stayed in a very old hotel. In the morning, it was very cold. As there were no geysers in the hotel room, they had to stand in line to get hot water to their bathroom in a huge bucket that the hotel supplied. They all had hot water baths and then went to the temple after breakfast.

The Sai Baba temple was lovely but Ganapathi was busy telling his sisters about his life at the boarding school. After prayers, they went back to the hotel. They stayed there for a while and left for Bombay after lunch.

Back from the Holidays – June 1969

On 10 June 1969, Ganapathi was back at his school and, this time, he was not as homesick as before. However, he still felt sad to watch Mama leave the school after dropping him.

This time, the games were football, cross country and gym. The boys had bought football shoes, which were heavier than their normal shoes and, thus, took some time to get used to.

There was this Sikh boy, Yogendra Singh, who always ragged Ganapathi. One evening, he pushed Ganapathi on the field, *"Why are you standing in my way?"* he asked and kept pushing him. Suddenly, Yogendra was flung up into the air and landed on his bottom. He was stunned and looked up to see Jimmy Parvaresh glowering over him. *"Why are you bullying him? He is smaller than you, why don't you push me instead?"* he asked. Ganapathi was surprised as Jimmy hardly spoke to him in the class. Yogendra got up but did not talk to Jimmy. *"I will see you in the dormitory"* he threatened Ganapathi and left. *"If he bullies you again, come and tell me, I will screw the joker"* Jimmy advised Ganapathi grandiosely and strutted off. He hated bullies and he never had that problem because he had Rustom, his elder brother, in the school.

The cross country run was fun and strenuous. The novices, that is boys aged 10 to 12 years, had to run around the cactus boundary; the juniors, that is 12 to 14 year old boys, had to run to Donkey Hill and then back around the cactus boundary, to culvert number 3. The intermediates, that is boys aged from 14 to 16 years, had to run up to culvert number 5. The seniors, that is over 16 year old boys, had to run up to culvert number 7. The race ended at Evans

Hall. The rains made the cross country run and football fun, and also difficult, but the students got used to it soon enough. Michael Bardey was the school football captain even though he was in the 10th standard and there were 11th standard boys in the team too. Hockey had the youngest school captain in Anil Puri, who was in 9th standard when he became the school captain.

The Rakshabandan Day – 1969

Ganapathi had four sisters at home. So, on Rakshabandan day, he was feeling a little sad, looking at his empty hand. At home, four bright big rakhis would have adorned it and he would have given each of his sisters a Cadbury chocolate from his shop downstairs.

He went to class after assembly and sat down quietly, reading his English text book. Rosemary kept turning around and kept looking at him. He did not notice her, as he was engrossed in reading. The boy behind him, Ravinandan Mohanty, hit him on his head with a book. *"What do you want?"* Ganapathi shouted while turning around angrily.

"I don't want anything from you, black man, but I think Rosemary wants something; she has been staring at you since she walked in", Mohanty clarified.

By now, Ganapathi was very fond of Rosemary, but she usually looked for him after the Mathematics class. He turned his attention away from his book and glanced at her.

Mohanty was right, Rosemary was looking at him and she seemed nervous about something.

The English teacher, Mr Michael, walked into the classroom, with his usual comment, *"You ready, fools; I am sure none of you have read the next chapter as I asked you to do"*. Ganapathi immediately said that he had read it twice. *"You are the exception to being a ready fool"* said Mr Michael, with a smile on his face. He pulled out his copy of the text book and started reading it out aloud. Then he asked questions from the story and explained the gist of the theme to a class that seemed more interested in the clock than his English lesson.

When Mr Michael walked out, Ganapathi got up and went to Rosemary, and asked, *"What happened, why are you looking so nervous?"*

"Can I tie you a rakhee?" she asked hesitantly. *"Of course, you can"*, he was elated. All morning he had been missing his sisters' attention on this day and here it was. Rosemary tied him a rakhee and the entire class clapped. That was the only rakhee that changed hands in this class and so they clapped. It was just a beginning. In the years ahead, more girls started doing this and in his 11th standard, Ganapathi would have 17 rakhees on his hand. After lunch, as he would have done in Bombay, Ganapathi bought his new sister a Cadbury chocolate, which she was very happy to receive.

Rosemary's pet name was Mamsu. She liked Ganapathi a lot but was worried that he would misunderstand her affection for something romantic, which it was not, and so she took this step to make him understand that the feelings that she had for him were only sisterly. After that, Ganapathi started calling her Mamsu and also met her for Brother's Hour on Sundays when the boarders usually used that hour as an excuse to meet their girlfriends. Mamsu's twin, Putsie, also became Ganapathi's close friend. They were his first female friends at Barnes. His friend among the boys was Kishore Thadani.

Dilip Rao - the Head Boy

The day of the cross country run dawned. It was a rainy day and the runners were very happy that they did not have to run in the sun. The youngest started first, followed by the juniors, intermediates and finally the seniors. The cross country points were that whoever had the most points lost. The first runner got one point and the last one got the maximum points, depending upon the number of the runners. Usually, around 60 students ran. The novices, juniors and intermediates came in one after the other. Royal and Spence houses scored the least points. All depended upon how the seniors race ended.

As expected, the Spence house captain, Dilip Rao, who was also the head boy of the school, came in first, with the second boy coming in after a long time. The winner had outstripped all of them very early in the race and held the lead to the end. Dilip Rao collapsed on the ground, with his chest heaving with the exertion of having sprinted up the slope from Gate Lodge. His victory also sealed Spence house's victory in the cross country championship. Royal house came in second; Candy third and Greaves came in last with the maximum points.

The morning study was on and Ganapathi wrestled with a Mathematics problem. He sat in the first row and his house captain, Dilip, sat on a desk in front of him. He was scared to ask him but, as he had to complete his homework, he disturbed him. Dilip was surprised with the question but being patient with the juniors was a part of his character. He showed Ganapathi how to do the sum and was favoured with a wide smile. After that, whenever he had a doubt about any sum, he never hesitated to ask his house captain for help, although his friend, Kishore, was puzzled, *"Don't know how you disturb him, I get scared even when he just looks at me"*.

The football series was won by Royal house. Gym was also won by Royal again, with Spence a close second because of two day-scholars - the Khambatta brothers.

Every year, there was a poll to choose the most popular student of the year. Usually, the head boy was disliked, as he had to maintain discipline. But Dilip Rao, in spite of being strict, was loved by all, as he was gentle with the younger boys and always helpful. This year, he was one of the candidates. As expected, he won with a huge margin. In celebration, the boys carried him to the swimming pool and threw him in. Then, they all jumped in too, wearing their khakis. Today, the MOD would not scold them for going to the pool without permission and also swimming with their clothes on. It was Dilip's day.

Ganapathi gets Injured

The 7 pm bell rang for supper and the boys started walking to the dining hall. Ganapathi walked with Kishore and they talked, as usual. Suddenly, Ganapthi was flung into the air and hit his head on an electric pole by the side of the road. His forehead started bleeding profusely. He fainted and Kishore started yelling in fright. Four seniors picked up Ganapathi and ran to the hospital. Mamsu saw that it was Ganapathi they were carrying and was worried.

At the hospital, Sister Misquita did not get hassled. She told the boys to put him on a bench and examined his wound. She applied some medicine and placed cotton on the wound, with some tape to hold it in place. Ganapathi said he did not want dinner and so she let him sleep. She told the other students to go back to the hall. They left.

The next morning, Jam Tin took Ganapathi to the army hospital, where an army doctor stitched his wound, without using any anaesthetic. Ganapathi yelled out for all his worth but to no avail. The army nurse who held him was very strong. He was told to come back in a week to get his stitches removed. He went back to the school hospital to rest.

One of the seniors, Richard White, came to see him in the evening.

"*I was the one who knocked you down, we were having a race*", Richard explained. He then warned Ganapathi, "*If you tell any teacher that I knocked you down, I will beat you up*". The evening before, Ganapathi had not seen the person who had knocked him down and now he knew. Kishore advised him to keep quiet. "*That fellow is a mad man*", he cautioned.

Fight with Afzal Khan

The school term was coming to an end. These holidays would be very short, only for nine days. These were called the Michelmas holidays, as St Michael's feast came at that time. Some of the boys stayed back, as they thought it was too short a period to go home and have fun.

Afzal Khan, like many other students in the dormitory, called Ganapathi '*Kaliya*'. Ganapathi did not mind when his classmates or seniors called him that. Afzal was still in the primary school but had been shifted to the junior dormitory because of his age. So he retaliated by calling Afzal 'piddler', referring to his habit of wetting his bed.

Afzal did not mind at first but when others also started calling him piddler, he was very angry with Ganapathi for starting a pet name. He threatened Ganapathi, "*I have it out for you Kaliya, just watch out*". "*What are you planning, piddler, going to wet your pants in class too*" was the worthy reply from Ganapathi. Afzal slapped him hard and Ganapathi punched him in return. Soon they were punching each other, as the other Spence house boys sat down to watch. Fights were always interesting. After a couple of minutes, Afzal sat over Ganapathi and held him down with both his hands. His feet were immobile because Afzal sat on them. *"Say you give up, Kaliya"* he taunted. Ganapathi jerked his body upwards to no avail; however, he refused to surrender. Another boy, Riyaz Hussain, stopped the fight and made Afzal get off Ganapathi.

"Kaliya, next time I will kill you", Afzal warned.

"Piddler, we will see about that", Ganapathi brushed him aside.

Wrist Watch goes Missing

Ganapathi wore a Favre-Leuba watch, which his father had given him when he first came to Barnes. One day, when he came back after taking his bath, he found it missing. He searched everywhere and asked all the other boys in the dormitory but nobody claimed to have seen it.

A month later, Barinder Katyal, while going to the toilet, noticed Salman's trunk was open and something shone in its lid. There were two strips of metal in the top lid to make it stronger, with a gap between the strips and the top cover. In that gap, something was shining. On checking, he found that it was the watch. He left it there and informed the house master, Mr Hoffman.

It was a Saturday and Hoffy promised Katyal that he

would do the needful and advised him that he should keep his mouth shut in the meanwhile. There was a rest period from 2.30 pm to 3.30 pm, during which the boys were supposed to sleep. Whether they slept or not, the prefects made sure they stayed in bed and were quiet.

At 3.15 pm, Hoffy came to Spence house and asked them to stand. During such time, all boys had to stand near their respective beds. Hoffy called Katyal and told him to start checking all the boys' boxes. Without much ado, Katyal took out the watch from Salman's trunk and gave it to Hoffy, who showed it to Ganapathi. It was his watch and Hoffy told him to wear it and be more careful where he kept it.

Salman went down with Hoffy. The boys started talking among themselves. Katyal told them what had happened. The prefects were shocked at this behaviour and chastened themselves why they had not checked and found the watch before Hoffy.

Salman was caned by Hoffy. He got six of the best hits on his bottom and he returned upstairs crying. Boys in the hostel started calling him *chor*. The bell rang and they all went down to have tea. By the 6 pm roll call, the entire school came to know about Salman's bad behaviour. He became a pariah, as in Barnes, only robbery of food was tolerated; in fact, praised.

On Monday, Salman had to meet the Principal, who warned him sternly that, as this was his first offence, he was forgiven. *"Next time, you will be thrown out of the school"*

Principal Davis warned him. He ordered him to go and meet the Vice-Principal Roberts, who also caned him; again it was six of the best. Salman wished he had never seen that watch.

The term ended on a high and it was time to go home, albeit for only nine days. Nair Mama came to take Ganapathi home, while Kishore went home with his father.

Afzal Khan Runs Away from School

The final term started with a bang, with teachers telling the slackers that if they did not pull up their socks, they would be repeating the class next year. This term had cricket, swimming and athletics as sports. Athletics were the most fiercely contested sport in the school.

The mile race was also looked forward to, as the 100 m sprint. There was a fierce competition in the house to get into the relay team. There were two teams, one team was for the 4 x 100 m relay race and the other team was for the 4 x 400 m relay race. This division was in every age group. As there were four age groups, there were eight relay teams and boys competed to make it into a group of 32 in a house of 64, which meant that half of the house was in the team. This did not include the day-scholars, but very few of them were interested in games.

The Khambatta brothers from Spence house were an exception to this rule, but they competed only in swimming, gym and diving.

It was the 6 pm roll call. One boy from Spence house, Afzal Khan, was found missing. The head boy, Dilip Rao, selected four of the best runners in the school and sent them to the railway station. *"The Punjab Mail leaves for Bombay at 6.45 pm, check it; he will try to get on it and keep a watch on the way, he might be hiding somewhere"*, were his instructions. They reached the station at 6.30 pm and asked the station master if he had seen anyone in Barnes school khakis. The station master checked with the ticketing clerk who confirmed that a boy had bought a ticket to Bombay and he was wearing khakis. They could not however find him on the station.

Afzal Khan had been hiding inside a toilet, as he knew that they would come searching for him. Just before the train came in, he decided to cross the tracks and get in from the other side, knowing that the platform would be watched. As he crossed over in the dusk, a dog barked nearby, which alerted the searchers who then ran in that direction. They saw him crossing and caught him. He kicked and bit them but to no avail. They carried him back to school and handed him over to Hoffy, the housemaster.

Hoffy looked at Afzal Khan kindly and asked him softly, *"What is the problem? You could have told me"*. Afzal started crying. *"Everyone calls me a thug"*, he replied, as he wept.

"I will tell them not to do that", Hoffy assured him and sent him upstairs to change. He also called the mess and told

them to send some food for him. Afzal came down to find dinner waiting for him outside Hoffy's house. He ate and immediately felt better. Next day, Hoffy called the prefects of Spence junior, Bhagwan Mirchandani and Ravinder Singh, and explained to them why Afzal had run away and what they had to do now to make sure that it does not happen again. The prefects promised to pass on his diktats to the other boarders. So the boarders of Spence house were instructed not to call Afzal a thug and they sniggered, but no one ever called him a thug again. They knew the prefects would beat them up if they disobeyed.

A Candy house boy, Kaisar Hakeem, came to the Spence house dormitory to call Ganapathi. It was a Saturday afternoon and they had just come back from lunch. Half of the boys were roaming around and the other half were fooling around in the dormitory. *"What happened?"* asked Ganapathi, the thin boy. *"Some visitors have come to see you"* he replied. Ganapathi was surprised, as Nair Mama had come only the previous week and that he would come next only after a month. But as visitors usually meant tuck and money, he ran down the staircase. It was his elder sister's husband, Kanagraj Nadar, and his dad's partner, Ramachandran Nadar. He was excited to see them and started doing a quick jig. His brother-in-law was amused, but advised, *"Stop it; the other students will think you are mad"*. *"I don't care Athan (that's what he called him), here I am known as a scholar and not a mad person"*, he boasted. It was true that he had topped his class in the first term examination.

Ramachandran Anachi (elder brother) asked him about the food. *"Horrible, everything is boiled, but we feel hungry all the time and so we eat, sometimes porridge with worms"*, he replied. Then his brother-in-law gave him a box of sweets from his favourite Banarasi sweet mart in Khar. *"You went to Khar to buy?"* he asked. *"Yes! Your sister, Dhanam, said you liked sweets from that shop"*, he replied. He then gave Ganapathi 20 rupees. *"Don't be such a kanjoos, give him 100 rupees"*, instructed Ramachandran Anachi. *"Are you going to give it to him or should I?"* he quizzed. Kanagraj complied and immediately gave him a 100 rupee note and, in return, Ganapathi did another jig. He ran after their departing tonga for a while and then stopped to enter the Tuck shop.

Ganapathi's Academic Slide & Second-term Sports

Athletics were strenuous, but each student practiced the event where he thought he had a chance to win a medal. Cricket was also played with vigour. Swimming was the only game where it was more fun and less competition. The good swimmers practiced while the others had water fights, ducked each other or just floated in the water.

In the previous (first) term examinations, Ganapathi had stood first. In the second term now, Vijay Banker had joined the class. He had been unwell during the first term.

As predicted by the other students, he stood first in the second term examinations. Ambika Talwar then joined the class in the third term and Ganapathi was pushed down to the third place.

In athletics, most of the events had heats, and the finals were held on one day. Some events though did go straight to the finals, like the 'mile race'. All the students liked the mile race, and it was fiercely contested. Mr Gama blew the whistle and the race started. The runners were bunched up for only the first 50 m or so and then the better runners broke free.

Dilip Rao raced ahead. His stamina was the best, as he had won the cross country race during the last term, but he was not as fast as some of the others. He knew he had to maintain a healthy lead if he had to win this one. In the last 400 m, the sprinters would try their best. Dilip Rao led the race for the first three rounds, covering a distance of about 1,100 m. At the beginning of the fourth and the final round, Douglas Kerr, the school's star athlete started increasing his speed. Knowing this would happen, Dilip also hastened his pace. Dilip was about 50 m ahead at that point. Though he ran as fast as he could, Douglas started closing in at an alarming speed. Spence and Royal house boys started screaming their lungs out. Douglas belonged to Royal house. At the 300 m mark, Dilip's lead was now reduced to about 35 m, and at the 200 m mark, it was only 20 m or so. At the 100 m mark, Dilip's lead had reduced considerably to only about 10 m or so and Dilip could hear Douglas literally breathing down his neck. Dilip gave it all he had and sprinted the last 100 m straight, cheered on by a hugely excited crowd. People sat on the edges of their seats and some jumped up and down. Both athletes started striding down the ground with only about 25 m to go. Douglas made a last desperate lunge and started closing on the leader.

When Dilip Rao breasted the tape, Douglass Kerr was only 5 m behind him. Dilip collapsed on the field, while Douglas watched him. Douglas did not collapse, he stood quietly. (Dilip was the head boy in 1969 and Douglas followed him in 1970.) Spence house erupted into a wild dance, as they carried Dilip around the ground. Florence Nightingale, the sister house of Spence joined in the cheering. After all, he was one of their own.

In the girls' athletics, Debra Dameron and the Phillips twins led in most of the events among the juniors.

Royal house again topped in athletics and Candy house in cricket. The swimming finals were amazing. Glenn Arnold, the Royal house captain, versus the Spence house Khambatta brothers set the pool on fire. In the intermediate group, it was Rustom Parvaresh of Royal house who led the others. In juniors, again, it was Royal house this time, led by the twins, Jimmy and Sharukh Parvaresh, who were Rustom's younger brothers. Royal house won the swimming cup too.

The year came to an end after the final examinations. There was a party for the outgoing 11th standard students. They also gave a party for their house and the rest of the students had bought them goodies. There were speeches and tears, and a lot of hugging and crying. The school head boy and the Spence house captain, Dilip Rao, could not hide his tears, as he related how he had come to this school years ago as a small boy, and how it had made him the man that he had become. His speech got the loudest cheers even though he was in tears. The food for the party was a mixture of chips and cold drinks. The boys enjoyed it.

The Bhusaval passenger rolled into Devlali station in the afternoon. The first two coaches were for the Barnes students. In the first coach, the girls and prep house boys got in; and in the second coach, the junior and senior boys got in. The MOD, Mr Gama, got into the second coach, while the teacher-on-duty, Mrs Michael, got into the first coach.

Dilip Rao made sure that all others had boarded before he gave the 'all clear' to the station master who waited for him. The station master waved his green flag and the passenger train started rolling with a loud and long whistle. In five minutes, they passed Barnes school, which was clearly visible on the right. The juniors were happy to see it go but, for those, who had just passed out, there were tears in their eyes.

New Term – New Students

Ganapathi arrived at the school accompanied by his uncle, Nair Mama, hoping that Kishore would have also come back. His best friend had promised him that he would leave the school as he hated the boarding life. His prayers were answered, as Kishore landed up with the other students on the Bhusaval passenger train.

Ganapathi had arrived by the Kashi Express train, which had come in an hour earlier. The boys were as boisterous as ever and the prep house boys, who had just moved upwards to the 6th standard, were the noisiest of all.

In the dormitory, Christopher Philips yelled out to his prep house mates. He was very good at games but not at all interested in studies. His elder brother, Keith, was in Greaves house and studying in the 7th standard, Section B Keith was a good boxer and good in games like his younger sibling.

Balasaheb Gawli and Kailash Sawant had also come up from prep house. They were from rural Maharashtra and their English accent was a delight. They were also very fun loving. Karim Merchant was their favourite for his story telling talent. His stories about fatty and skinny people were the toast of the dormitory on the weekends.

Satinderpal Singh Sachar was another boy who had come up from prep house. He was very mischievous and always full of fun. He frequently got into fights with other boys but always became cheerful in a little time.

The prefects had warned Kareem that he could not tell stories during the week days. He could bring the dormitory to a standstill, and also late night nobody slept, as they listened to his stories where he had a different voice for every character.

Ganapathi had a sister living in Kalina, Bombay. She had a shop there. Next to her shop was a saloon whose owner, Raghavan Nair, was from Kerala. Her husband, Kanagraj, and Nair were best friends. Kanagraj told Nair that his brother-in-law was in a very good school in Devlali and, therefore, he should also send his four kids there. Nair became very happy with this plan, as he had a small house behind his saloon and it was difficult to live in that small accommodation with his four kids. So, he and Kanagraj visited the school. Raghavan liked it and then admitted his four kids there - his daughters, Nailini and Pushpa, in 6th standard; his son, Ashok, in 5th standard; and his youngest daughter, Usha, in 2nd standard. Ganapathi introduced them to his friends as his country cousins.

Kareem had two younger brothers studying here. One was in Candy house and the other was in Greaves house.

The morning 6 am bell rang and Mrs Banks, the matron, started her rounds waking the boys up with a ruler, with which she banged the metal beds with a song *"Wake up boys, wake up.... "* The boys just snuggled in further into their blankets. She came back at 6:15 am, but it was finally the prefects that got the boys out of bed.

Hunger Pangs

At 7 am, they rushed to study in the Gym hall annexe. Most did their homework and some fell asleep. The MOD, Mr Paul, usually woke the sleepers up with a tight slap but today he just tapped them. Another teacher had cautioned him that when you hit a sleeping person, sometime the student could die of fright. Mr C Paul's younger brother, J Paul, had joined the school that year. He was a bachelor and well dressed, and a braggart. But for the students, he was fun and a great music teacher. He also told long stories about how he came to a class when a teacher was on leave.

Ganapathi and Kishore would generally feel very hungry. The bun, banana and tea at 4 pm would not be enough to fill their stomach. One day, the Tuck shop man had still not come. They got tired of waiting for him and so they walked to the berry bush in front of Spence block. They started throwing stones at the berries, as the bushes had grown quite tall. Soon they had a pile of berries. They divided it into two lots and ate their share.

While they ate the berries, some sweet and some sour, but nevertheless manna for two hungry young boys, the Tuck shop man suddenly turned up as they finished the berries.

A crowd shouted at the Tuck shop man, who seemed to be used to the noise. He served the seniors first and then the juniors. His name was Hemnani but the kids called him Sayi, which is a Sindhi word. They were two brothers; the elder one was called Bada Sayi and the younger Chota Sayi.

The two friends had their normal two samosas with a mangola. That day was Kishore's turn to pay and so he paid. They took turns paying on alternate days. But they never changed the menu. They just loved the combination of samosas with mangola.

The Seventh Standard (1970)

A Part of Football Team

THE 7th standard was not much different from the 6th standard, the only difference being the teachers. Ganapathi had by now been pushed down to the fourth place from the first that he had achieved in his first term at Barnes, however, he did not let this bother him. He was trying to be good at games and it was beginning to hurt that he was never chosen by any team in any game. He practiced hard and his house captain, Michael Bardey, noted his efforts at every game. But he was simply not good at sports. Michael knew he was very intelligent but he seemed not to use his brains where games were concerned.

Michael took some time out to teach Ganpathi football,

following which he was soon good enough to be in the D team of Spence house. When he got his coloured T-shirt for his first game, he cried because he was very happy. His team captain, Christopher Philips, made sure to play him in a position where the ball went rarely. Christopher was very fond of Ganapathi as a dormitory mate but he did have his shortcomings as a footballer. Kishore came to cheer him. Kishore was not in any team but that did not bother him. *"Next year I will not be here, so who cares whether I am in the team or not"*, was his regular consolatory statement. He really hated the boarding school though he was now beginning to get used to it.

Ganapathi had become Mr Hoffman's pet. When there was a water shortage, he had to go up to the roof to check the water level in the tank. One had to go up by the fire escape at the back of the building. He felt very important doing this. If the water level was less, the boys were told not to have a bath but only wash their hands and feet instead. This happened frequently in summer. The prefects made sure that no one broke this rule. They were worried that if they ran out of water it would be hell to use the toilets.

Food Thief

Mrs Banks was furious. Someone had robbed her dinner. She called the prefects from the two dormitories on her floor and warned them that if this did not stop she would go and complain to the Principal. The prefects knew that they would not be able to the food thefts easily, so they decided to watch the boys carefully and catch them red handed. It would certainly be more than one boy, that they were sure. Boarding boys always shared the spoils, particularly food.

They announced that someone was regularly flicking the matron's food and that person would be severely punished when caught. Surprisingly, it stopped immediately. It was Mr Hoffman's pet, Ganapathi, who was the culprit, otherwise being a peaceful student. Usually, he would never rob anything. But on that particular day, as he felt very hungry, he had eaten the matron's dinner, which comprised just two sandwiches.

One day, Kaisar Kumar Dupaishi, who had come to the junior block from prep house that year, went to the tuck cupboard in Mum Banks' home. There he saw his dormitory mate Ganapathi eating biscuits and also checking out the other stuff in the cupboard. *"You want something - ask, stop robbing"* said Kaisar severely. Ganapathi was shocked. He did not know it was Kaisar's stuff that he was checking out.

Just to try him out, Ganapathi asked Kaisar, *"Why don't you let me taste the jam biscuits?"* Kaisar gave him two biscuits. Ganapathi was surprised and happy. He gave Kaisar a couple of biscuits and a sweet. They became friends after that.

Kaisar was from Tibet. He was a year junior to Ganapathi and a very well behaved boy. Barinder, Manoj and Sunil were friends. Michael Bardey, the house captain, frequently called them together with a shout *"Suri-Mittal-Katyal"*, as they were always together.

Sunil Mittal did not like Ganapathi and frequently bullied him. One day, Harish Jawahar saw Mittal bullying the smaller boy. *"What is your problem, why are you bullying a smaller boy"*, he demanded. *"Because you cannot bully a bigger boy"*, was the insolent reply. Harish punched him so hard that Mittal fell down. After that, he stopped bullying Ganapathi or anyone else for that matter. Ganapathi was touched, as Harish was not his friend.

Spence juniors' prefects were Ruallah Naimi and Asad Asadi. Ruallah was a six footer and Asad was a tough man. One afternoon, Mr Hoffman had gone to town and he had instructed Mr Gadre to keep an eye on the boys.

Saturday Afternoon Wresting in the Dormitory

On Saturday afternoon, as a rule, from 2 30 pm to 3 30 pm, boys had to stay in bed. It was called the 'rest period'. The boys were in bed when Ruallah decided to have some fun. He told the juniors that they had to wrestle with a boy across the dormitory in front of them. The wrestling started. The boys were happy, as normally the rest period was boring. They did not notice Mr Gadre coming in, who was horrified to see them wrestling and the prefects were refereeing the duels.

Mr Gadre yelled, *"STAND"*. The boys froze. He slapped every boy hard and those who ducked got two hard slaps. He threatened the prefects that he would deal with them later. They felt lucky that he had not slapped them. Next day, both prefects lost their job and went back to Spence block. Two other seniors were made the prefects for the rest of the year.

The junior boys always looked forward to the monthly movie at Cathay cinema, which was inside the Artillery center. After breakfast, they lined up outside Evans Hall and there was a roll call. After the roll call, the junior boys marched first, followed by the seniors. They were two abreast and anyone breaking formation faced hell from the prefects who were very attentive once they left the school premises.

They knew there were guava trees on the way and the boarders would not let go of an opportunity to pluck a few even if the owners objected. The prep house kids and girls were taken to Cathay by the mini bus, which was fondly called Jam Tin.

Saturday Movie at Cathay

Once they reached Cathay, there was another roll call to make sure nobody was missing. Even then, after this roll call, a few seniors did go missing. They had gone to the Deviali bazaar to eat and returned to the dark theatre before the lights came on during the interval. It was an English movie, black and white, from the World War I times. But the boys enjoyed it. This movie was better than no movie.

During the interval, there was a scramble for the burgers,

which were famous at Cathay. They were hot and oily, and crispy, and the students loved them. The girls could not get into the canteen, as it was too crowded. The girls gave money to their friends among the boys to get them burgers, which cost 50 paise in those days. It was a bun which contained a sliver of meat.

After the interval, followed by a burger and a coffee, which cost 25 paise, the rest of the movie followed. Ganapathi had 10 paise and Joseline Gomes from Greaves house had 15 paise left after burgers. They bought a coffee together and shared it. In Khar, Mumbai, they lived very close to each other and often saw each other during the holidays.

The walk back to the school in the hot sun wasn't as enjoyable as the walk to the theatre. It was like going back to a jail as the students said. They went straight to lunch as the lunch time was an hour late. After that, they went to their dormitory to sleep off. In the evening, they played as usual. It was after all a Saturday.

In the evening, Mr Hoffman called Ganapathi and told him to check the water level. He went up feeling important. Christopher Philips also wanted to go and so he took him along. *"When I go to Spence block, you can check the water level"*, said Ganapathi. Once they were on the roof, they checked the view in all directions, particularly, Broken Tooth, which was the highest peak in the western ghats visible from their school. Once in the past, some students had climbed that peak and had shone a mirror reflecting the sun's light on the school, signaling that they had reached the peak. There was enough water in the tank and the boys were happy. Bathing was a pleasure in the summer months. It felt horrible when they were allowed to only wash their hands and feet when there was less water.

Ganapathi's Sweetmeat

On Thursdays, the boarders used to get one sweetmeat with their dinner. Someone would steal Ganapathi's sweetmeat every week. He complained to Mrs Jones, who was then the in-charge of the mess. She replaced it and the following week, she kept a close eye on Ganapathi's plate while the boys came in for dinner.

Firoz Barot from Spence house, an 8th standard boy, was the culprit. She caught him red handed and slapped him hard. She returned the sweetmeat to Ganapathi and said, *"It was your house boy, Firoz"*. Later in the dormitory, Ganapathi followed him. *"I always knew you are a pig and now you are a thief too"* he said loudly. Other boarders looked on with interest, as it looked like a fight was brewing. *"Your father is a thief"*, Firoz retorted. *"He is not a boarder here, you pig. You want a sweetmeat, beg for it, I will give it to you, but don't rob"*, reprimanded Ganapathi.

"You want me to beg from you, black man", said Firoz, feeling insulted. *"First let me give you something"*, he added, as

he punched Ganapathi. Soon they traded blows. This lasted for a few minutes and ended with Ganapathi falling flat on the floor and Firoz sitting on top of him and raining blows. The prefects stopped the fight and warned Firoz, *"Next time you rob anyone's food in the mess you will get beaten up by us"*.

Raksha Bandhan Day

A day before Raksha Bandhan, Kishore and Ganapathi had their usual snacks at the Tuck shop. After that, Ganapathi bought a Cadbury chocolate. *"This is for Mamsu, tomorrow she will tie me a rakhee"* he told Kishore. *"I am an only child, so only my cousins tie me rakhee"*, Kishore replied.

The next day, as expected, Mamsu did tie Ganapathi a rakhee in the morning 15-minute break. Then her twin, Putsie, came and also tied Ganapathi a rakhee, followed by his two other classmates, Debra Dameron and Corrine Fernandes. In the lunch break, he went and bought Chocolates for all of them.

Hole in the Bathroom Door

Mr Walsh's classes were the most interesting, as he had a habit of enacting whatever he taught. Mr Russel was a serious teacher and never joked with his students, nor ever floated away from whatever he taught. Walshy (Mr Walsh) taught English literature and Chappiya taught Mathematics. They had just come back from class and were changing into their khaki clothes when their matron, Mrs Banks, came screaming out of her house. She was yelling and saying something, which no one understood. Mr Hoffman came out of his house, looking alarmed. *"Mrs Banks, calm down"*, he shouted but to no avail.

In the Spence house dormitory, Ganapathi slept closest to the door and saw the matron first. He came running out and ran straight into the matron's home, thinking it must be a rat or a snake that must have upset her. There were no such creatures around. He came out and asked her what was wrong. Finally, after calming down, she led him into her bathroom, behind the house. There too, he could not see anything out of place. He looked puzzled. She pointed at her door. It was a huge wooden door. At a certain height on the door, a hole had been drilled neatly through it.

"Someone has been watching me bathe", cried Mrs Banks, pointing towards the hole, and let out a loud wail. She looked like she was going to faint. By this time, a prefect had come in and he led Mrs Banks to a chair, and made her sit down. He glared at Ganapathi and ordered, *"Go tell Hoffy about what has happened here"*. Ganapathi went down and told the story to Hoffy, who looked shocked. He immediately called the attendant and sent for a carpenter available in the campus. The hole was closed in the next hour. Students discussed the hole at tea time and soon the entire school knew. Boys were snickering and saying, *"She is an old lady; this guy must be a starved sicko"*.

The Spence house boys had a suspicion about who it was but nobody said anything. Omerta, the code of silence, was as strong in boarding school as it was among the Mafia.

After the games ended at 6 pm, the boys went up to their dormitory when Hoffy made them assemble before his house. *"Number one, I am shocked at your behaviour at this young age. Number two, I am sure you are not going to tell me. Number three, I want to assure you that if I find the culprit he will be dismissed from school"*, he announced. Mr Hoffman had a habit of numbering all his statements as he felt the students would remember better. He did not know that the students called him *"Number One"* because of this habit.

The hole drilling did not happen again and was soon forgotten as a dirty prank. As Ganapathi was the one who used to go up on the roof to check the water level, he was the only one who was on the fire escape staircase regularly. Hoffy asked him if he saw any of the other students on that staircase. *"Christopher is the only one who comes with me as I am training him to take over when I go to the senior block"*, replied Ganapathi seriously. Mr Hoffman hoped that this would not happen again, as it was dirty. The biggest crime here was usually stealing food, which was not taken very seriously. But this was really bad, he thought.

The year passed and soon they were on their way home. This year, Micheal Bardey and his batch-mates passed out from Spence house.

The Eighth Standard (1971)

A New Girl in the Class

STANDARD EIGHT had a new girl. She was very pretty and her name was Bernadette Brown. She was a very quiet girl and not very good at studies. She was good at games. She had half the boys in the school in love with her in a few weeks' time. Ganapathi was totally infatuated with her, but he never told her that. He was scared that she would stop talking to him. She, like all the other girls in the class, approached Ganapathi when she could not figure out a Mathematics problem.

One day, Mr Walsh (Walshy) was teaching the class 'Julius Caesar' and he was enacting the assassination scene where Caesar gets murdered. Walshy played Caesar and the students had to stab him. Ganapathi was Brutus and when he stabbed him, Walshy screamed, *"Et tu Brutus, then die Caesar"* but not before leaping up and down in a frenzy and then falling flat down.

The students looked worried, as they thought he might have hurt himself with that fall but Walshy was perfectly alright. He explained to the students how to fall on your hand without getting hurt. For the rest of the period, all the boys tried it and many got badly hurt in the process. After the period got over, the boys continued to try it in the field and in the dormitory till they got it right. Walshy was truly an inspiration for the boys.

Syed Ali Hussain was now the new school head boy and also the Spence house captain. He was a boy who was fair to everyone and rarely got angry. Normally, he never shouted at anyone. Syed had a younger brother, Riyaz, in Spence house. Riyaz was very proud that his elder brother was the head boy and also his house captain. Riyaz did his best to improve his boxing and playing skills, but he never bothered about studies.

Daniel Bardey was another Spence house boy who was very mischievous. He was also good in games and poor in studies.

Playing Cards in Blind Well

It was a Sunday evening; the Brother's Hour was over and the boys had returned to their part of the school. Senior boys were in their recreation room and the juniors were milling around. Riyaz, Daniel and Ganapathi went to the blind well and sat down in its center, at the bottom. They had hidden their playing cards there. They played flush with money. The MOD, Mr Louis, had seen them going in that direction, expecting them to be running around the blind well, but had wondered how could they run with their leather shoes, full whites and ties on.

When he could not see them running, he became curious and decided to go down and check himself. There was no smoke and so they were not smoking. He was shocked to see them gambling. He confiscated their cards and the money, and asked them to stand outside Spence block. Riyaz was scared that his elder brother might see him; Ganapathi was worried that Mr Hoffman would see him. Only Daniel was not bothered. He waved to the boys who looked at him.
At 7 pm, the bell rang for supper. All the students went there except these three. They stood there forlornly.

Mr Louis knew that Ganapathi was a very good student and Riyaz a very good sportsman; only Daniel was the mischief maker in the group. He decided not to take the matter any further. He told them to join the others for supper. They ran to the mess happily.

The Debate Evening

After dinner on Saturdays, they usually had free time till bedtime at 9 pm, but on that evening, it was the debate.

It was Candy versus Spence. Actually, the girls' house was also part of the team. There were two boys and two girls in each team. Spence house, as its partner, had its sister house Florence Nightingale.

All the students above 8th standard had to attend the debates. The topic was *"Is Reservation Helping the Country?"* Spence and Nightingale houses were speaking for the motion, and Candy and Joan of Arc houses against the motion. The speakers were given 5 minutes each and there was a warning bell after 4 minutes. They lost points if they spoke longer. After all the speakers had finished, the debate was thrown open to the house. Some boys and a few girls went up to speak their minds. Richard White from Spence house always went up to speak. He had always something funny to say and the students loved him.

Ganapathi had observed the earlier two debates but at this one he wanted to speak. He had a written speech, which was for 50 seconds, as he knew he had only one minute. He spoke with a lot of hesitation and his hand was shaking. Students seemed to realize that it was his first time and so they gave him a patient hearing and clapped very hard. He was thrilled. Mamsu waved out to him when he looked in her direction. Bernie mouthed well-done when his eyes met hers across the hall.

Spence and Nights won the debate and also the debating cup that year.

Ganapathi Loses his Keys

The next day morning, they woke up at 7 am, as it was a Sunday. After breakfast, they played various games. Ganapathi was worried. He could not find his keys. He searched all over the ground in front of Candy block but to no avail. He asked all his dormitory mates, class mates and friends, but no one had seen his keys.

Ganapathi had an interesting keychain. It had nine small knives attached to it. Ganapathi knew that the knives would be hard to resist for most students even if they did not use his keys. His classmate, Tarun Vyas, who the students called 'Polson', because he was fat, observed him keenly. *"You lost something"* he asked. *"Yes my keys"* Ganapathi replied. *"What reward are you giving the finder?"* Tarun wanted to know.

Ganapathi knew that Tarun had found his keys and smiled.

"You can keep the knives, just give my keys back", Ganapathi pleaded. *"Are you sure, you won't ask for it later?"* Tarun quizzed.

"I will not, now give me my keys" Ganapathi assured confidently. As he had anticipated, Tarun pulled out the keys from his pocket and separated them from the key chain. He returned the keys to a happy Ganapathi, who then went immediately to the canteen and bought another keychain, a simpler one.

Soon the holidays were on them. Ganapathi did not have his Nair Mama to take him home this time. He went home with the other boys by the Bhusaval passenger train, singing and dancing all the way.

Return from Term Holidays

After the holidays, Ganapathi returned by the Nagpur Express train, which had many students in it. At Kalyan station, while they were buying edibles, a TT accosted them. Mohanty did not have a ticket. Ganapathi had bought the tickets for four students who had found him standing in line in Dadar and had given him money for their tickets too.

Ganapathi showed the four tickets to the TT and he was satisfied. At Igatpuri station, Mohanty went out with one of the tickets and bought two tickets to Devlali. The train stopped for 20 minutes at Igatpuri. At Devlali, the TT collected their tickets. He was not interested whether they came from Mumbai or Igatpuri; all he needed was a current ticket to Devlali. The boys took tongas to reach the school.

Building Repairs after a Cyclone

When they reached the school, they were shocked. Candy block, Spence block, Haig-Brown and Lloyd block had only part of their roofs left over them. The rest had blown off. There were roof tiles lying all over the place. A cyclone had struck the previous night. If the students had been there, the damage could have been frightening, with a lot of injuries and perhaps deaths, but God had been merciful.

The school was closed indefinitely for repairs. As it had happened the previous night, they did not have the time to inform the students, though the Bhusaval passenger train students were sent back from the VT station.

The students left their luggage in their dormitory. The first floor dormitories were fine and the second floor dormitories were out of bounds for the fear of falling tiles. Mrs Banks said that she would stay back in the school, she was not going anywhere. Ganapathi felt sorry for her and gave her a couple of biscuit packets he had bought for his tuck box. He could get more when he came back. Mrs Banks was very touched.

They returned to the station by the same tongas and boarded the Punjab Mail train at 7 pm. By midnight, they were home, telling the stories to their amazed parents, who were happy that the students were not in the school when the cyclone had struck.

Most of the items for the roof repairs were purchased from the family shop of Abdul Lateef Chowdhury, who was a student in 8th standard. The repair work took three weeks to complete. The students received a telegram on a Friday to return to the school.

Ganapathi's father insisted that he leave immediately, though he wanted to leave a day later, on Sunday. So, he left reluctantly. There were very few boys coming in on that day. As he had thought, some came on Saturday but most returned on Sunday.

Saturday School

On Monday morning, Principal Davis informed them of what had happened that night and that no one was injured. He said during that term, there would be classes on all Saturdays to make up for the three weeks lost. The students groaned loudly, but he gave them a stern look though inside he was smiling.

Even the teachers were not happy with the Saturday school, but they would do their job as usual. On the first Saturday, they followed the Monday timetable and on the next, they followed the Tuesday timetable, and so on. They continued like that till the lost three weeks were compensated; with such schedule lasting the whole term.

An Inter-school Match

It was the term for football, cross country and gym. The students played hard and tried to study hard. They had an inter-school match with Boys Town, Nasik. Kumar was not in the team, but he came with the cheering squad. He was Ganapathi's first cousin. While the rest of the school watched the match, Kumar was in the canteen with Ganapathi, who had taken him there for a treat.

Barnes won the game. Mr Gadre saw them coming back from the canteen and enquired as to how Ganapathi knew this Boys Town student. He was happy with the explanation. *"I say, man, why isn't your cousin in Barnes?"* he asked. *"I don't know"*, replied Ganapathi.

Kumar went back with his school mates. He would see his cousin in Mumbai during the holidays now. He had two other brothers, but he was the only one in the boarding school. He had a married sister who lived in Nasik and he went there on the weekends.

Ganapathi in Love

Ganapathi felt he was falling in love with the new girl, but he never told her. He spent as much time with her as possible whenever she asked him to help her with Mathematics or some other subject. The boarders knew and teased him often, but the girl did not know. She, of course, knew that he had a crush on her but never mentioned it.

The Marriage Jinx

During the earlier term holidays, Mr Hoffman had married the Hindi teacher, Miss Oliver. So, she was now Mrs Hoffman. As Miss Oliver, she was very strict but surprisingly, as Mrs Hoffman, the housemaster's wife, she was very sweet to the students. The boys were surprised and, among themselves, they said that Hoffy had a very good effect on his wife.

Ganapathi thought about his 6th standard teacher, Mr Michael, who had married another teacher. The marriage lasted only for a year, as Mr Michael had passed away. He hoped that nothing untoward would happen to his favourite teacher and the house master. Sadly, what he had thought did come true. It was not Mr Hoffman, but his sweet wife who passed away. Their marriage had also lasted for a year. There was some kind of jinx in Barnes when teachers married each other, said the boys. Those that came married to Barnes were doing fine.

A Swimming Pool Fight

The boys loved going to the swimming pool but it was very difficult to get permission. One had to have a senior boy to ask permission and he had to be a life saver, and the senior boy was allowed to take only a few junior boys with him. So, usually, a group of seniors got together and took permission first for themselves and then for the juniors that wanted to come along. They would go down to the pool at around 10 am, but had to be back by the 11.30 am roll call on Saturdays and Sundays. They could not go before that, as breakfast was over at 8.30 am and students were not allowed into the pool for at least an hour after eating.

Ganapathi had gone down to the pool with Rustom, who led them. While they were down there, the boys were happy swimming, racing, throwing water at each other and ducking each other. Rustom allowed only those seniors, who were also good swimmers, to go into the diving pool. He did not want to risk any accident here. Many a time, juniors had jumped on a swimmer from the diving board, causing serious injury.

On that day, Ganapathi, who was swimming slowly, found himself being ducked. He thought it was a senior and tried to get away. When he turned around, it was not a senior, but his junior from his own house, Rafiq Charania. He was shocked and felt insulted. How dare a junior duck him? He slapped him hard. As they were wet and in the water, the slap stung and was really painful. Ganapathi got out of the water, as he knew Rafiq would fight. In the water, there was no escape. He planned to change and go back to the dormitory when Rafiq hit him. He boxed him back and soon it was a free for all. Rafiq was a street fighter and soon bashed the other boy up.

Rustom, who was watching till then, saw that others were just watching and having fun. He was alarmed when he saw Ganapathi bleeding from his nose. He knew him to be a serious student and would not start a fight. He stepped in and held them apart. When Rafiq tried to shake loose, Rustom warned him, *"Don't make me hit you"*. Rafiq was alarmed.

Rustom could easily beat him up and, moreover, he had two twin younger brothers, Jimmy and Sharukh, who were known fighters. They were watching with interest. One more word against their elder brother and they would make Rafiq regret starting a fight.

Being prudent, Rafiq calmed himself and threatened

Ganapathi, *"You come to the dormitory, will teach you a lesson"*. With this ominous threat, he stormed off. Rustom instructed Jimmy, *"Take him to the canteen and put some ice on his nose. If that doesn't stop the bleeding, then take him to the hospital"*.

Drowning Accident in Diving Finals

It was the day of the diving finals. Parvez Razvi of Candy house was easily the best. In the junior section, Surjeet Singh Kheer of Candy house came onto the one metre board and executed a perfect dive. But once in the pool, he started drowning. Sister Misquita's son was the nearest to the pool. He was a powerfully built boy. He jumped in and carried Kheer out. The boys were shocked.

Mr Gadre was amazed at how this boy, who did not know swimming, in the diving team? He gave the Candy house captain an earful. *"How the hell did you not know that he doesn't know swimming? Has he practiced diving in your presence? How did you select him in the team?"* he shouted.

Kheer stood looking sheepish but not at all bothered by his near mishap. He knew there were many boys who would save him but he was also sure he knew swimming. He wondered what worked in the middle school had not worked in the diving pool. He had to find out if there were different strokes for the diving pool. Mr Gadre glared at Kheer, *"If I ever see you anywhere near the diving pool, you will get six of the best on your bare bottom"*. That scared Kheer.

The Car Accident

Soon the second term ended and the school took a small ten day break with the Michaelmas holidays. A few students stayed back because the holiday was too short. The third term sports were cricket, athletics and swimming. It was also the time for studies, as the final examination would be held in November.

Ganapathi planned to go back to the school by train when, suddenly, he got a call from his brother-in-law, from Kalina, who informed that the Nairs were driving to the school and he could go with them if he wanted. Ganapathi's father was not keen on this arrangement, but he agreed, as his son seemed to be interested in accompanying them.

They left from Bombay after lunch and were on their way slowly through the Ghats. It had become dark and they planned to stay at Nasik that night and reach the school the next day.

As they were traveling, a truck coming from the opposite side suddenly dashed slightly towards their car and went on its way. At that moment, the car driver had his arm hanging outside the car, which got smashed by the truck. He stopped the car with great difficulty. The girls started crying when they saw the blood. Mrs Raghavan tied up the driver's hand hand as tightly as possible. Another car going to Nasik agreed to give them a lift. They went straight to the Government hospital where driver was admitted. They stayed in Meher Bakery hotel, which belonged to the Haghighis from Barnes.

Ganapathi was very happy to see Mosadique Haghighi there, as he was called 'Daddy' by the whole school, including some of the teachers. Rustom was also there. Ganapathi told them about the accident.

The next morning, Ganapathi, along with Mosadique and Rustom, looked for their car, which they had left outside a house on the road. After they found the car, Mosadique drove back in his own car, while Rustom drove Nair's car to Nasik. At Nasik, Mosadique found another driver to take the car back to Bombay after dropping them to school. The injured car driver looked better when they visited him in the hospital before going off to the school.

As they had arrived late at their school, they had to first get permission from the Principal before going to their dormitory. All of them stood silently, while Ganapathi, the eldest among them, launched into a detailed story about what had happened the previous evening. Mr Davis listened gravely and asked only one question, seemingly relieved that his students were not injured, *"How is the driver now?"*

"Much better, his hand is plastered now", they replied.

After Mr Davis gave them a signed slip, they went to their respective dormitories. Once in the dormitory, they started relating the story of the accident to their friends, who were happy that nothing more serious had happened.

The Final Term

The girls to Haig-Brown, the younger boy to prep house and Ganapathi to his block on the boys side. Most students started studying in this term only. Ganapathi got through with minimum studies but sometimes thought about the days when he had stood first in the class. It appeared to be so long ago. It made him sad but he made no effort to study hard.

He was in the 'D' team in cricket and trying to get into the 'C' team. In athletics, he was trying to make it to the 800 m race, as he was not fast enough to participate in the shorter races. In hurdles, he realized he could not even jump over the low hurdles.

The 11th standard students became sad as the days passed. It was time to say goodbye to the school that they had begun to love so much. They would miss the place and they would miss their dormitory mates the most. Class bonds were not as tight as the bond among the boarders.

The year ended. Syed Ali Hussain, the school headboy, delivered a tearful speech in Spence seniors' dormitory. There were tears in the eyes of the juniors too. They had eaten the snacks that the outgoing students had bought. They had also given gifts to the seniors who were leaving that year.

The Bhusaval passenger train rolled into Devlali station. The first two coaches were empty and locked. They were opened at Devlali. The first coach was meant for prep house and the girls, and the second one was for the boys of Barnes school. They boarded the coaches making a lot of noise, flinging in their iron trunks, as if they wanted to break them. They had loaded the girls' trunks first, as Mr Gama had ordered.

Ganapathi got into a coach, trying to get a glimpse of Berine in the crowd. He could not see her. He consoled himself, saying that he would meet her at VT station. A few students got down at Kalyan and Thana. Many got down at Dadar station. Mr Gama made sure that parents had come to collect them and, if not, instructed a senior to look after them till the parents arrived or they were supposed to escort them home. The seniors would follow this rule perfectly.

At VT station, all the students got down. Mr Gama and Mrs Micheal had to stay for the night at their sister concern, Christ Church, at Byculla and return the next day to Devlali. Ganapathi said goodbye to Berine with a smile, but he did not ask her where she stayed. He would be meeting Mamsu in the holidays. He would also meet Suri regularly and sometimes Kamlesh Jagoowani and Ravinandan Mohanty at Matunga during the holidays.

The Ninth Standard (1972)

Return to the School – as Senior

GANAPATHI DID not take the Bhusaval Passenger at 5.30 am in the morning. Instead he took the 7 am Kashi Express, which reached Devlali an hour before the Bhusaval passenger. He found many Barnes students scattered all over the train and soon they were a motley crowd. On the way they passed the Bhusaval passenger and had some fun shouting across the tracks above the noise of the two trains. The Bhusaval passenger had stopped to let the Kashi Express pass. They saw the school on the side of the track and sighed. Four months of jail time starts, they thought. At Devlali station, some of the boys and girls caught tongas and made their way to school. Some boys decided to enjoy their last hour of freedom. They left their luggage in the waiting room of the station and went to Devlali market for a meal.

When they came back, the Bhusaval passenger rolled in. Two compartments, as usual, had been reserved for Barnes and the students disembarked noisily. The Kashi Express boys joined them in the school bus that first took the Prep house boys and girls, and then the remaining senior boys. Jam Tin made six trips till all the students were in the school.

The first thing was a roll call to check the arrivals and the missing students. It was a Sunday. The MOD was Mr Emmanuel, who was the quietest of all the teachers. He taught biology and chemistry to the senior classes only. Generally, he had a bemused expression and ignored whatever the students were doing. He let the prefects do their duty. After the roll call, they went to their dormitories, helping each other carry their heavy trunks up the stairs.

Ganapathi was now in Spence block, which was meant for the seniors. It was a new feeling. In the junior Candy block, they had been the biggest boys, and now in the seniors' dormitory, they were the smallest boys. It was humbling, as well as a bit scary. He hoped there would be no ragging.

The senior boys block housemaster was Mr S B Gadre. He was much more strict than the genial Mr Hoffman and most boys were very scared of him. He had a habit of starting every sentence with, *"I say man...."* Thus, the boys called him 'I say man'. In the junior block, Mr Hoffman always read all the letters before giving them to the boys. Mr Gadre did not do that. He gave them their letters unopened. The boys appreciated this.

Ganapathi came to the senior block along with his other dormitory mates, Bharinder Katyal, Manoj Suri, Kamlesh Jagoowani and Christopher Phillips who was still in 8th standard. In the dormitory, there were a few students from the Middle East - Majid Badri, Aqeel Badri, Suleiman Mohebi, who were very good in football. Majid Badri was so good that, when he was in 8th standard, he was already in the first eleven of the school.

Then, there was Sharad Ved from Tanzania. The Arab students were spread in all the four houses. When they first came to the school, they knew only Arabic and Urdu, which helped them to speak in Hindi. After a few years in Barnes, they spoke English like the locals. They were favourite with the other students, as they brought more tuck than others and always had a lot of money to spend, which they shared with everyone.

Strong Goalkeepers

Among the Middle Eastern students was Shahab Fikri in Royal house, who was a gentle giant. He was extremely strong. One day, when he was the goalie in a hockey match, the ball came to him at a great height and at a very fast pace. Normally, the goalie would stop it with his gloved hand but not Shahab. He took the ball on his chest and did not even shrug while the rest of the team went *"WOW".*

This sporting incident became famous throughout the school till Mr Gadre warned him. *"I don't want any tom foolery. You could have broken your ribs. You are wearing gloves. You could have stopped the ball with your hands. You can take a football to your chest, but not a cricket or a hockey ball. Is that clear? Or do I have to ban you from the rest of the matches?"* he reprimanded Shahab. Shahab realized that his house master was really angry and also realized that he was trying to protect him. *"Yes Sir! I will not repeat that",* he said apologetically. Mr Gadre nodded grimly. *"You better not",* he said ominously. He went in shaking his head, thinking these Arab students were rockers.

Another famous goalie in the school, Harbhajan Singh, also belonged to Royal house. Harbhajan was huge in size for his age. He was the house goalie in both hockey and football. It was nigh impossible to get the ball past him in both games. Very soon, he was the goalie of the first eleven in football. For hockey, it was Shahab Fikri. Both were from Royal house, much to the consternation of the other houses.

The New School Term

On Monday morning, it was difficult to wake up at 7 am. Mum Peron, who was the matron here, was a gentle soul; she did not scream like Mum Tully or Mum Banks in the junior block. She knew the seniors would be dressed on time irrespective of the time they woke up. As it was the first day of school, there was no study from 7 am. The studies would start the next day when the rising bell would ring at 6 am to groans and cribbing.

At 8 am, they were lined up for breakfast. Mr Gadre was the MOD and so everyone was on time. The headboy said grace and they sat down to eat. Boys strained to see if their favourite girls had come back after the holidays. Ganapathi blushed when Bernie waved out to him. She knew he would have been looking for her. She had not been either in the Kashi Express or the Bhusaval passenger yesterday and he had been sad. She had actually come by the Nagpur Express, which leaves Dadar at noon and reaches Devlali at 4 pm.

At the school assembly, Mr Davis welcomed them back and they sang the first hymn of the year. *"Oh God our help in ages past our hope for years to come, our shelter from the stormy blast and our eternal home…"* The 9th standard classes were in Candy block and Ganapathi was in class 9th A. Most of his classmates were there. Nothing had changed. Bernie smiled at him and he felt very happy to be back in school. He had missed her during the holidays.

Their class teacher was Mr C Paul, who taught them English. He also played the piano at the morning assembly and at church. He was very strict and smiled rarely. As he was their class teacher, he was a little lenient with class 9th A.

The first day of the term was spent in familiarizing with the new time tables, receiving text books and note books. They had to buy brown paper to cover all the books. So the next day went in that exercise. The normal classes started on Wednesday.

A Strange Hindi Teacher

Mr Gupta engaged their Hindi class and also a vocation class. Mr Hoffman did not take any of their classes, but Ganapathi was happy to meet him every week at the Scouts meeting. Also, when Mr Hoffman was put in-charge of making hymn books, he assembled a team, which included Ganapathi. He was excused to make those books for one period a day. The pages had been printed. They had to first arrange them separately. Then they had to assemble each book with 40 hymns. After that, they had to stitch the book together with two covers. This took a month. At the end of the month, Mr Hoffman gave them a party with lots of cakes and wafers. The boys were happy.

For some reason, the Hindi teacher, Mr Gupta, took a dislike to Kitchie Attawar even though the boy had polio in both his legs. Kitchie was a very good student and stood second in class, but was very mischievous. One day, he kept talking back to Mr Gupta, who became so angry that he caught Kitchie by the collar and shook him like a doll. The class was shocked to see Kitchie being manhandled. Seeing the pained looks of the other boys and girls, Mr Gupta let him go with the words, *"You better behave yourself"*. Luckily, Kitchie kept his mouth shut. Like his classmates, he too was stunned. No teacher had ever struck him.

A Weekly Food Relationship

During the first term, it was hockey, swimming and boxing. The games were on. Ganapathi managed to get into the 'C' team by virtue of being in the 9th standard and not for his capability in the sports. In boxing, he won his first bout against Jeffrey Gomes of Greaves and lost the next bout to Hazrat Ali Patel, who was in Royal house. They did not hit each other very hard, as they were classmates in Class 9th A. Hazrat's cousin, Iqbal, was in Spence house and very fond of Ganapathi. He had told Hazrath to go easy.

Ganapathi was known as a scholar and not a boxer. Ganapathi decided to study hard, as he was not making any headway in the games. He managed to win the Science and Mathematics Prize at the annual prize day. The last time he had won a prize was in the 6th standard, when he used to stand first in his class.

On Sunday evenings, there was Brother's Hour after tea, where boys were allowed to meet girls. Most of it was romantic, though there were also a few brothers and sisters in the school. Ganapathi used to go to meet Bernie, as she also enjoyed his company. The Brother's Hour was from

4 pm to 5.30 pm and, after that, the boys had another hour and a half to kill till supper time. Ganapathi went to the canteen to eat something. At the same time, Sharukh Parvaresh also entered. He was the elder twin of Jimmy, who was Ganapathi's classmate.

"What are you going to eat?" asked Sharukh. He always had a mischievous twinkle in his eyes, as he was up to something. He also had a very innocent smile. *"Samosas and Mangola"*, Ganapathi replied.

"Why don't you try the laganshala, it is a tinned vegetable and we can eat it with bread", Sharukh said. *"I don't have that much money"*, Ganapati replied.

"No worries! This week I will buy and next week you buy" said Sharukh. Ganapathi was surprised, as he was his senior, but he was his favourite mentor Rustom's younger brother; so he agreed. They bought one tin of laganshalla and one packet of bread for which Sharukh paid.

The Tuck shop man opened the tin with a tin opener and gave it to them. They walked away from the crowd to sit on a septic tank, which was on the way to the swimming pool. They shared the bread first and then sat down to eat. *"We should have bought a drink too"*, they realised.

The next week, it was Ganapathi's turn to pay and, thus, this habit of sharing a laganshalla started and lasted through the entire year. And another astonishing fact was that, apart from this weekly food relationship, they never interacted through the remainder of the week for anything else. An amazing friendship only for eating and only on Sundays!

The New Privileges

Being in the 9th standard meant a lot of new privileges. They could now go out with market permit once a month, which meant leaving the school at 8.30 am and come back for the 11:30 am roll call. Then, there was a monthly day permit, where one could come back for the 6 pm roll call. There was also an extra movie at the Cathay or Adelphi theatres. One could also attend the dance, which took place every term. Now, the students really felt like seniors.

That Saturday was their first market permit and the 9th standard students were excited. After breakfast, they lined up outside Evans Hall. The MOD, Mr Gama, checked the boys against the list given by the prefects. There were 40 students. He let them go.

They walked towards Haig-Brown, talking among themselves, when one of the boys shouted, *"Hey! There is a bus coming from South Deolali"*. Hearing this, the boys sprinted down the road, as they knew the next bus would not come for an hour and, therefore, they would have to walk to Bagur to catch another bus. As it was downhill, they ran easily. The girls outside laughed. The girls were lucky. For their market permit, they could use Jam Tin to go to market and come back. They also had a teacher accompanying them.

The fastest sprinter reached Gate Lodge first and stopped the bus, which waited happily till all the boys boarded the bus. Once they reached Devlali market, most of them rushed to a small restaurant called *"Maulana"*, which served non-vegetarian food. It was popular for *keema chapathi*.

After that, they went to a sweet shop, Mathura Dairy Farm to eat, and then returned to Maulana for another round of non-vegetarian food. Finally, they got down to shopping, which was largely food stuff for the people who had not come to the market, as they were still in lower classes.

All the 9th standard students had come, but not all the 10th and 11th students had come, as they had found the market permit was too short and, thus, preferred to go out on day permits only. For the day permit, the boys went to Nasik. For this, they had to catch a second bus from Devlali. There they watched two movies, as there was nothing else to do the whole day. Most of them had lunch at a restaurant Meher Bakery owned by the Haghighis of Barnes school. If If Papa Haghighi, whose children were at Barnes, would be sitting at the cash counter, the Barnes students could expect free lunch. He just waved them away in a fit of affection for the school.

After the second movie finished at 6 pm, ten boys huddled together in an Ambassador cab, to be able to return to school on time for dinner. They were an hour late, but

Mr Gama did not shout at them; he had heard about the two movies day permits long ago. Girls did not get day permits.

The Easter Ball

In the first term, the first dance of the season was during Easter; it was called the Easter Ball. It took place on the night of Easter Sunday. It was a holiday for the students on Monday too. As it was a four day weekend, starting Good Friday, some students even went home for a short holiday.

The boys and girls were all dressed up smartly. Again, one could see some nervousness and excitement in the 9th standard students. The students from the two senior classes, however, looked relatively much more relaxed. The boys and girls sat all over the place in little groups. A boy played a Beatles' song on an old record player. The Master of Ceremonies, Mr Walsh, invited the head boy to start the dance by inviting the head girl for a dance.

Syed Ali Hussain went to the head girl and politely asked her for a dance. They danced to a slow number, Englebert, and then they split. The head boy would choose another girl while the head girl would ask any other boy to dance with her.

For his second dance, Syed naturally went to the prettiest girl in the school, Bernie Brown, and asked her for a dance. After that, she went and chose Ganapathi to dance with her. He did not know how to dance and she spent the next hour teaching him the simplest fox trot.

The boy who was a genius in class was a bumbling idiot on the dance floor. She had fun teaching him. He was just excited to hold her hands. The dance ended at 10 30 pm. They had started at 8 pm after dinner.

Monthly Movies

Every month, the entire school went for a movie to Cathay, where the entire theatre was booked for Barnes. For the second movie for seniors, however, they could not book the entire theatre. They went for a regular movie at 6 pm. Jam Tin made two trips to the theatre for the boys and girls. Two teachers accompanied them.

The movies were usually very old English movies, but if it was a western movie, the students loved it. One of the movies that they watched was *Mackenna's Gold.* Another movie was *The Good, the Bad and the Ugly.* They also watched a few Bud Spencer & Terence Hill movies, which were called the *Trinity Series.*

The First Pair of Spectacles

The first term came to an end and the students went home for their summer vacations. They came back after a month and a half. Ganapathi wrote to his father, saying that he could not clearly see the blackboard in the classroom. His father wrote to Mr Davis. After assembly, while he walked out of Evans Hall, Mr Davis called Ganapathi and also Mr Paul.

"Where does he sit in class?" Mr Davis asked Pauly.

"The girls sit in the first three rows and he sits in the fourth row", Pauly replied.

"You cannot see the writings on the board?" he asked Ganapathi.

"No! Sir", Ganapathi replied.

"Then you must go and see an eye doctor on Saturday", Mr Davis instructed.

On Saturday, Ganapathi told Mr Gadre, the house master, that he had to go get an eye check up. Mr Gadre gave him a note for the MOD. Ganapathi went to Nasik to meet the eye doctor, who treated all Barnes' students. He checked his eyes and found that he needed glasses. His number was found to be .75 and the glasses were ordered in the same clinic. The good doctor told him to return at 6 pm on the same evening to collect them. Ganapathi went and saw a movie. He also had lunch at Ali's restaurant, where as expected Ali would not charge him any money. Thereafter, he collected the glasses and felt a little odd wearing them, but he did wear them.

Back to Being A Scholar

Ganapathi was very happy when his friends told him that the glasses made him look like a scholar. He wanted to be a scholar. In the 7th and 8th standard classes, he had tried his hand at sports but had failed miserably. So, he had decided to go back to studies with a vengeance. It wasn't easy, as he had dawdled for two years after being a topper in 6th standard.

In the classroom, he could now see the blackboard clearly and, accordingly, wrote to his father that he liked his new glasses. As it was the first term of the new school year, hockey, swimming and boxing were the games being played.

The English class was in the post-lunch session in 9th A classroom. Mr Paul conducted a particularly boring class. In a fit of mischief, Ganapathi yawned loudly to show off his boredom. Mr Paul got very angry. He marched up to Ganapathi, removed his glasses and gave him one tight slap. He then replaced the stunned student's glasses. Ganapathi was shocked but the other students laughed loudly. They loved the fact that Pauly had removed his glasses so as to not break them.

In the Spence seniors' dormitory, 30 students lined up opposite each other on iron beds, with coir mattresses. Two extra beds lined up perpendicular to the others at the one end of the dormitory. These two beds were for the house captain and the vice-captain. In the juniors' dormitory, these two extra beds were for the prefects.

Next to the house captain's bed, there was a wardrobe for students to hang their clothes on a metal pipe. On another pipe, there was a curtain to protect the clothes from dust. Students hung their blazers and their Sunday whites there.

Hockey was played on four different fields. The 'A' team played in the athletics' field outside the swimming pools. The 'B' team played in the ground parallel to it on the other side of the shed, where the students sat and watched athletics. The 'C' and 'D' teams played on a field outside Evans Hall.

Swimming was held in three pools and they were below the Hill. Boxing practice was undertaken in a shed next to Candy block. The first few bouts were also held there on a temporary stage that had been put up. The finals of the boxing were held on a stage outside Evans Hall.

Evans Hall

Evans Hall, where the assembly was held every day, was huge. The entire school could be accommodated there, with plenty of space still left. At one end on the first floor, church services were held. On the ground floor was the mess, where the whole school could eat at one time. Each table had one house, which meant 32 people could eat, with the house captain and vice-captain seated at the head of the tables.

On one side in Evans Hall, was the Tuck shop and, on the other side, was a biology lab. The post office was also in this building, and the teachers also had a billiards room in this versatile building. The PT finals were held on the first floor in this hall, as also the gymnastic finals.

The dormitories were housed in huge stone buildings, which had two floors; each floor had two dormitories. In the middle of the building, between the dormitories, was a house, where the matron lived. There was also a huge storeroom, where the students' clothes were kept.

The tuck box was inside the matron's home. Number '5' was a building at a little distance behind Spence block. It had the school library and also classes of 6th and 7th standards, both divisions. Candy Block and Spence block had classes on the ground floor. The housemasters also lived on the ground floor. Next to the house master in Candy block was the residence of Hindi teacher, Mr Gupta. In Spence block, along with the house master, lived the Marathi teacher, Mr Bhalerao, who the students thought looked like the smuggler, Haji Mastaan; both had similar moustaches.

The Principal lived above his office. Across from here was the school hospital where sister Misquita resided. A doctor came in one day a week. Serious cases were sent to the Artillery Centre hospital, which always took care of Barnes students, particularly, when they hurt themselves on the playing field. Students who needed a dentist would go to Devlali and those who needed an optician would go to Nasik. Anyone who came down with any serious disease would be sent home.

The 9th standard was much more difficult than the junior classes that they had been through. The syllabus was much more elaborate and the students would start studying hard quite early in the terms. Earlier, they would study hard only during the last week before the examinations. Bernie and Ganapathi had become good friends but he was sad when she told him that she would not return to the school next year, as she had found the studies very difficult. Half of the class comprised girls and most of them had tied Ganapathi a rakhee, as he had helped them in Mathematics. The 9th standard classroom was in one corner of Candy block. It had 45 students and their class teacher, Pauly, was happy with them. There was a very popular student, Rustom Parvaresh, who was the house captain of Royal. He took a liking to Ganapathi and they became friends.

James Bond Movie

It was a Saturday and they had the whole day to do as they pleased. But even then, the students were restless. Daniel Bardey had heard from the day-scholars that a James Bond movie was being played at Cathay and he had decided to watch it that night. After asking half the dormitory, he found two people to accompany him. After dinner, they went upstairs at 8.30 pm to change into their night clothes. The three students in Spence house senior block, who had decided to bunk that night, were Daniel, Kailash Sawant and Babasaheb Gawli. They made dummies in their bed, so that a cursory glance would show that someone was sleeping there. Then they tied two bed sheets together and climbed down from a rear window. They wore their night clothes.

Going to the movie in the school uniform would have given them away at first glance. No one would know who would phone the school if they saw them. After climbing down, they walked downhill towards the swimming pool. Then they went through the servants' quarters and walked out of Gate Lodge. Those days, there were no watchmen.

Once on the road, they talked normally and walked to the theatre, as no bus was available at that hour. They reached Cathay and the theatre was crowded with army folk, as it was a weekend. People from Devlali camp had also come to watch the movie.

The movie started at 10.30 pm. It was a fun movie, with lots of action and skin show. The boys loved it. In the interval, they had two hotdogs each. The movie finished at 1 pm. The canteen was still open, so they bought another hotdog for the way home. Munching on it, they started walking back to school. Once they reached Gate Lodge they stopped talking. On reaching their block, they called out gently, but to no avail. Then they whistled and yet there was no response from the first floor. They picked up small pebbles and started throwing them at the windows.

At that moment, incidentally, Mr Gadre was just about to go to the bathroom. He heard the pebbles. So, he quickly put on his night gown and went outside, opened the door to the building to check and then went upstairs. The noise seemed to have come from Spence house. As he entered the dormitory, he heard another pebble landing inside. Thereupon, he woke up one of the boarders, who almost died out of fright seeing Mr Gadre in the dark. *"What do you have to do?"* he asked.

"We have to throw down two bed sheets tied together" he whimpered. *"Okay, throw it down"*, Mr Gadre ordered. The shivering student hung the bed sheets down. Gawli was the first to climb up. He shrank in fear on seeing his house master, but did not say a word. Sawant was the next to climb up, followed by Daniel, who was pulling up the bed sheet when he felt a cane on his backside. He shrieked and the dormitory started waking up. *"I say, man! The rest of you sleep peacefully, you three come with me downstairs"*, Mr Gadre said very softly. His voice was silky soft and yet scary.

"You have a market permit, day permit and two movies a month. Not enough for you great people, it seems! I am now canceling all your privileges for the rest of the term, and now bend down" he announced as a judge. Each of them got six of the best from Mr Gadre's hardest cane. Their bottom would have become sore for a week and they would have found it difficult to sit. Mr Gadre did not inform anyone but he would have brought it up at the teacher's meeting on the Wednesday morning. The other teachers had agreed that the punishment was enough and that they need not do anything more. The Principal, Mr Davis, had also felt it was enough, but he added, *"If they repeat the outing, we will*

have to dismiss them; it is dangerous for the students to be out in the night and we are responsible for their safety".

Post-movie Fights and Retributions

Though they were punished by the house master, the trio became heroes overnight amongst the students. Everyone agreed that someone had to be awake at Spence House to throw down the bed sheets, but without the pebbles they would not have been caught. Babasaheb Gawli thought that someone had ratted on them and accused Ganapathi, *"In Junior block, you were Hoffy's pet and spy, and now you are spying for Gadre also."* he shouted. Retributions!

Ganapathi was surprised at this accusation, which was not true. Moreover, Gawli was his junior, so how dare he talk to him like this, he thought. Ganapathi became very upset and challenged Gawli. *"Yes, I am his spy, what are you going to do about it?"* he demanded. Gawli was shocked at this open challenge but, surprisingly emboldened, he proceeded to beat the hell out of Ganapathi, shouting, *"Teacher's chamcha, chugli khor, carrying tales".* Ganapathi was knocked down and fell on the floor; Gawli was kicking him hard.

Riyaz stopped Gawli and said, *"Ganapathi would never carry tales; I know him for four years".* *"Then why did he say yes?"* demanded Gawli.

"He is my junior; how can he talk to me like this?" Ganapathi protested, while still in tears. Riyaz first scolded

Gawli and then, to make Ganapathi feel better, he slapped
Gawli but after first winking at him. Gawli took it in a good
spirit because he too did not want to make Ganapathi cry.
Making a senior cry was not accepted, as it was risky. If
the seniors decided to teach him a lesson, he would be in
deep trouble.

Gawli stood quietly, but his friend, Kailash Sawant, did
not like it. He had not seen the wink before the slap. *"Who
are you to slap him?"* he demanded of Riyaz. *"You keep out
of it"*, Riyaz replied. Sawant protested, *"You are allowed to
interfere with Ganapathi and Gawli, but I am not allowed.
Tu kya bade baap kaa aulaad hai kya?"* Riyaz was not the
one to be cowed down; he slapped Sawant, who retaliated
with gusto. Another fight started. This was a fight between
equals and five minutes later they were still fighting. They
did not see Mr Gadre walking into the dormitory.

"I say, man, isn't the boxing ring in the gym?" he said in
his most sarcastic tone. He gave a withering glance to the
Captain and Vice-Captain of Spence house, *"Are you both
here to maintain discipline or watch the fun?"* They hung their
heads in shame. *"Both of you come down"*, he demanded of
Riyaz and Sawant, and walked down. Nobody told him
about Gawli and Ganapathi, and the two worthies were
spared a caning, but not the ones who had interfered. Riyaz
and Sawant got caned. *"Best of three should suffice, as both
are alive"*, said Gadre, as he caned them hard.

"Next time, Gawli, even if you kill Ganapathi, I will not interfere", said Riyaz, when he came back after receiving punishment from the house master. His bottom was on fire. Sawant echoed his statement, *"Riyaz, you can slap Gawli as many times as you want, mera baap ka kya jaata hai"*. He held his bottom and tried to soothe it with a gentle rub but it just aggravated the pain.

Gawli let loose a string of abuses at Ganapathi, *"Blackie, you caused all this"*. Riyaz gave Ganapathi a warning glance and mouthed, *"Don't reply"*. Ganapathi did not reply, but showed Gawli the *"up yours"* finger. The prefects had just been warned by Mr Gadre about not doing their duty. So, it was a tense situation. If Gawli started something new now he would receive it back from four hands. Gawli knew that well, as he saw the House Captain looking at him angrily. He shut up and started tidying up his bed.

Guava Farm Visit

It was a Saturday and the boarders were restless. Satinder Sachar, Daniel Bardey and Christopher Phillips had decided to go and visit a guava farm not far from the school. They went down past the blind well and continued till they came to the cactus wall. They found a breach in the wall and crawled out carefully.

The cactus was capable of cutting them up badly if they brushed it. They entered the guava field and started eating the biggest and the ripe ones. Once they had satisfied their hunger, they started gathering a few to take back to their school. Unfortunately, they did not see the farmer till he almost reached them. Christopher and Daniel were very fast runners. They were gone in the twinkle of an eye, but not Sachar. He was shocked to see the farmer and he froze in fear. The farmer caught him and put him in the pump house room. He then latched the room and decided to go to the school to complain. The farmer did not know that the boarders would never desert their own.

Both Christopher and Daniel kept a watch from a safe distance. The farmer got on his bike but then abruptly changed his mind. He came back to the pump house and put a lock on the door. He went to Barnes school to meet the Principal and to give him a piece of his mind about how to control young boys. Once the farmer was out of site, both the boys went back to the guava field and spent the next 15 minutes teasing Sachar about what Mr Davis would do to him when the farmer came back with school staff in tow. After 15 minutes, they decided to let Sachar out, as the farmer might come back any minute. They saw the lock was huge and could not be opened or broken. So, they simply broke the latch, which they had done on numerous occasions in the past but on trunks when they had stolen snacks. After Sachar came out, they found a goat nearby, which they caught and latched up in the pump house. Then they ran back. They knew there would be a roll call once the news reached the school.

The farmer went to the Principal and complained that the school boys had been robbing him all summer, and only today he had been able to catch one out of the three thieves. He also informed him that he had locked him up. The alarmed Principal went to the office attendant and ordered him to go and bring back the boy. *"I will punish him harshly and he will never come back to your farm"*, the Principal assured him. 'Six of the best and his two associates will get it too', he thought.

The farmer and the attendant soon reached the pump house. The farmer was shocked to see the broken latch and yet he could hear some noise coming from inside the pump house. He opened it and the goat ran out. He realized that he had been hoodwinked and did not say a word.

Mr Davis smiled when the attendant told him that they had found a goat in the pump house. On Monday morning, after the prayers had been said and the hymns had been sung, Mr Davis first announced the games for the evening and then continued, *"Magic has occurred in our area. In a matter of half an hour, a student of Barnes has turned into a goat in a nearby farm"*. Sachar, Bardey and Phillips almost died trying to suppress their laughter. Many boys who knew the story started laughing. The girls looked puzzled; they heard the story when they went to class later that day.

"*I know that you think you are smart but you are disturbing the farmer's livelihood. First, you cannot leave the school without permission. The second sin is robbing. The farmer has promised me that next time he will take you straight to the police station and not come to the school. We will not bail you out and your parents will have to come down here to meet the cops. So think about that next time you choose to be adventurous*", Mr Davis concluded.

He knew his speech would have not much effect on the boarders but he still had to warn them.

In their class that day, the three became stars and soon all the teachers knew their names. None complained but in the next staff meeting, Mr Davis was given their names. He too did not do anything. Boys will be boys, they all thought.

Donkey Hill Fire

It was a Saturday afternoon, after 2.30 pm. The rest period was on and all the boys were on their beds. Some of them had fallen asleep. Christopher Phillips went to the bathroom. When he came back, he looked out of the window towards Donkey Hill. He saw smoke rising from the grass beyond the quarries. "*Fire, Fire*", he yelled and promptly ran out of the dormitory. A few boys followed him and started running towards the high grass, which was burning merrily. "*Fire, Fire*", the shouts grew louder. Some of the smarter boys started running down with buckets, which they filled with water in the toilet behind the Junior block at the back.

Soon, the entire junior block of over a 100 students gathered in the open. Mr Hoffman was shocked to see his boys running out. *"It was the rest time, so what the heavens was happening"*, he wondered. At that time, he was wearing his pants but only with a vest. So, he quickly wore a shirt and his socks. He was not the one to go out without being properly dressed. 'One needs to set an example', was his motto.

One of the Candy house boys, Kaisar Hakeem, had taken off his khaki shirt and started beating the fire. Others followed suit. The fire was not under control at all. No one thought of calling the fire brigade at Devlali or the neighbouring Artillery Centre for help. Mr Hoffman came and saw his students beating the fire with their shirts. *"Stop that immediately"*, he ordered and made the students form a line from Candy block to the fire. One boy was filling the bucket with water and passing it down the line. Hoffy asked one more boy to fill water. Only two boys were allowed to throw the water on the fire. The rest just stood in line passing the water and the empty bucket back to the fillers.

In half an hour, the fire was put out. Mr Gadre, hearing the commotion, had come to see what happened. *"Must be the smokers"*, he told Mr Hoffman.

"It was the rest period", Mr Hoffman replied. *"The fire*

must have caught earlier when the boys would have gone there to smoke; they must have thrown the cigarette butt, as usual. You must have seen the fire during the rest period. Doesn't it mean it caught fire at the same time?" he concluded. Mr Hoffman did not argue. He was relieved and happy that the fire had been put out.

On Monday morning, at the school assembly, the Principal, Mr Davis, announced, *"There was a big fire at the back of Candy block within our boundaries. It was put out by Mr Hoffman and his boarders from the junior block. We are proud of them".* Everyone clapped and Mr Hoffman beamed. Among the seniors, a few looked sheepish. They had been smoking near the quarries before going upstairs for the rest period. No one could recall whether they had stubbed out the butts.

Mr Gadre noticed the sheepish looks and thought he had caught the culprits. When the seniors came out from the assembly, he remarked, *"I say, man, smoking is a crime but the bigger crime is not putting out the butt."* The boys looked alarmed but, with great effort, kept their faces blank. If they showed any sign of guilt, they knew that their house master was capable of beating the hell out of them. They kept walking. They could feel him staring at them hard but they just kept walking till they reached their class. They thought, *"Thank God! We don't have Physics today; can't say what 'I say man' will do in the class".* They did not smoke for a week after that. And next time, when they smoked, they threw their cigarette butts into the water in the quarries.

Unsporting Sportsmanship

As it was the third term, the main sport was athletics. There was a new boy in Royal house, Michael Scott, who was very good in sports. Ganapathi whinged to his dorm mate, Surinder Katyal, *"All the good sports guys are put in Royal house. That's why they win so many cups"*. It was not true, as students who joined were rotated through each house.

Michael was very good in sprinting and he was also known to be very mischievous. He had joined the previous year and the first thing he did was to label Ganapathi a *"coal miner"*. Ganapathi ignored him for he was a senior and not in his house or class.

It was the 200 m heat for the seniors and one of the runners was Michael Scott. He sprinted around the bend and realized that he had left all others far behind. He laughed and then waited for them. When they caught up with him, he started sprinting again and again left them far behind. He thought he had done something great but Mr Davis was very observant. He looked very furious. He picked up the mike and announced, *"Athletes, you have to give your best irrespective of how the others are doing. It's not a circus comedy that you stop halfway like a clown and then laugh at others like an ass. Any further behaviour like this and you will be thrown out of the games".*

Michael Scott went red with anger but he kept his mouth shut. If he was thrown out of the games, his House Captain would probably kill him. The House Captain was very angry, but, as he was also the head boy, Ali Akbar Haghigi, he did not say anything on the field. But when he got to the dormitory, he made the boys stand and announced 'under market' for Scott, which meant Scott had to run in the middle of the dormitory from one end to the other.

The boys stood on either side and were ready to hit him with their hands or with their towels bundled up or stinging, depending on the individual boys. Michael Scott was alarmed but he knew what he could do. He waited for some time and then charged down the hall at full speed, twisting and turning towards the boys, instead of getting away from them. Before the confused boys could react, he had traversed the whole way. But it was a lesson for him; after that he never fooled on the athletics' field or any other field.

The annual prize distribution day came. Ganapathi was getting a prize after 3 years. He had swept the prizes in 6th standard, but faltered during the next two years. This year, he got the prize for Science and Mathematics, which would put him in the Science section next year.

Diwali Dance

For the annual Diwali dance, the ex-students had come for their annual reunion. The boys and girls had to vacate one dormitory for them. The students shifted to the other dormitories for three days.

The ex-students came on a Thursday and left on Sunday. They slept in the dormitory and ate with the current students. The dance was dominated by the ex-students. Usually, it was the head boy and the MOD who took charge. When the ex-students attended, one of them was usually the MC for the dance. It was always Munnu Hussain; he had graduated in 1960. He had a habit of reminding people that he was Vinod Khanna's senior. Vinod had gone on to become a successful film star. The head boy, Syed, did not mind, as he was fond of Munnu and thought he was being funny.

When the elections for the most popular boy in the school were held, there were no surprises. As expected, Rustom Parvaresh won; in fact, he got all the votes. He was such a nice boy and responsible too. The boys, as was their habit, carried him to the swimming pool and threw him in. Then, they jumped in after him, some in their khakis, some took off their shirt and some took off their pants, and some even jumped in naked.

Mr Gama was the MOD. He smiled, as he saw the multitudes rushing to the pool. 'Any excuse to jump into the pool', he thought. But, he was not worried, as he saw a lot of seniors had jumped into the pool with the students. 'They won't allow anyone to drown', he thought wryly.

Clothes Gone Missing

It was a Sunday morning and four students had gone for a swim to the pools. The pools were being cleaned, and so there was no water. This did not bother the boys. They just took off their clothes and jumped into the well that supplied water to the dormitories. After a while, three of them came out. One of them, Khusru Irani, said he would swim a little longer, as it was very hot outside. The three others tried calling him but finally left without him. Khusru, from the Candy house senior block, came out after half an hour. He could not find his clothes. He searched through the bushes but found nothing. He could not hear the customary giggle that would have been there if the boys were hiding nearby.

Not finding his clothes did not bother Khusru. He just walked up the Hill to his dormitory stark naked. Many students saw him but were not surprised. He was known to be a mad cap. Khusru was lucky that none of the staff saw him. Khusru was not bothered about the staff; the only one that scared him was his house master, Mr Gadre.

He once saw Ganapathi talking to Mr Gadre and asked him later, *"He talks to you nicely but he never talks to me; only beats me up regularly"*, said Khusru. *"You are such an angel*

and you never do anything wrong; how come he beats you?"
Ganapathi asked innocently. *"Haha"* Khusru laughed *"Now you are being sarcastic like 'I say man'"*, he said.

General Knowledge Paper Stolen

There was only one paper left for the whole school. It was the General Knowledge (*"GK"*) paper. Mr Russel taught GK to the 9th standard students. He had gone for a movie in the evening. One of the students, Jimmy Parvaresh, saw Mr Russel going away.

Mr Russel lived on the same floor as the students, by the side of the Matron. Jimmy knew how to open the lock in the front door of his house. Another boy kept vigil. He went in and found the GK papers lying on a table. He took away one paper and bundled the rest neatly. He also saw there was cake on the table. Being a boarder, he could not resist and took the cake too. He went into Royal house after locking Chapiya's house, which was Mr Russel's pet name, as he had a habit of applying lots of hair oil and combing his hair flat. He first finished the cake and then gathered his classmates. Without the rest of the students knowing, he showed them the question paper. They marked the questions in their text books and started learning the answers.

The paper was shared with students of Candy, Spence and Greaves houses too. Ganapathi instructed the students that they should not take their text books to the hall. He also advised them that they should not finish their papers quickly and they should not laugh or smile in the hall. He had made a copy of 100 answers without the questions in the right order. He had to share it with the love of his life and his other classmates in Haig-Brown. At breakfast, he signaled Bernie to meet him upstairs. Bernie was puzzled but decided to meet him. He was a serious boy and would not call her without reason. She met him on the first floor of Evans Hall, above the mess. *"These are the answers to today's GK paper. Share it with your classmates and then eat it up. Make sure you don't get caught with it"*, he instructed her. Bernie was stunned, as he was the best student in the class. 'Why was he cheating?' she thought, but did not say anything. She went downstairs, gathered her classmates and shared the information. It was to their credit that the rest of the school did not know what was going on. The day-scholars also got the information when they arrived.

Mr Russel was surprised when all the 9th standard students completed their papers in 15 minutes. He knew ten students could perhaps do it, but not all of them. Something was clearly wrong. He went out and collected all the GK text books that he could find outside on the staircase landing. The boys had not listened to Ganapathi's sane advice of not taking their text books to the hall, and not finishing the paper quickly. Russel found that all the text books had the questions marked clearly. He was stunned. He did not go back to the hall. Instead, he walked to the Principal's office and informed him about what he had found. Mr Davis was not as shocked as Mr Russel had been. He came back to the hall with Mr Russel and waited for the paper to get over.

"I have an announcement to make; all students will be carrying their desks back to their classroom this afternoon, as the papers are over. The 9th standard students will, however, not do that; they will be appearing for one more examination tomorrow. The GK paper will be held again. I know the boarders are supposed to be going home tomorrow, but the 9th standard students will not go home tomorrow. They will go home the next day", Mr Davis announced. His face was grim and he almost growled, *"Any questions?"*, as he glared at them, daring them to ask him.

The students did not look into his eyes; they were shocked, but did not complain. They had done something wrong and were only getting back their due. So the next day, when the rest of the school left for their holidays, the 9th standard students stayed back. Mr Russel set another paper and announced before the start, *"Mr Davis has told me to cut ten marks from all of you, so the highest marks will be 90, and not 100. I usually deduct one mark for a wrong answer, but today I will be deducting two marks"*. No one even bothered to look at him.

After the paper, as they were walking out, Ganapathi went to Mr Russel and asked him gently. *"Sir, will you get angry if I ask you a question?" "No! Ganapathi, I know you would have got centum yesterday and today, and you will not do anything like this, please ask"*, he said. *"How did you know that we had got the paper?"* he asked.

"Everyone finished quickly. I went out and checked their text books. The questions were marked clearly in all text books. And then I suspected something last night and today it was proved right", he replied. *"Suspected what and why?"* asked Ganapathi.

Mr Russel laughed and explained, *"I did not notice that one paper had been removed, but as I had a cake on the table, which had gone missing, I knew someone had sneaked into my room. Now I know it was a standard nine boy".*

Ganapathi went back to his friends and told them, *"I told you buggers not to take the text book to the hall, but you still did it. Plus, you idiots also finished fast, even though I had specifically told you not to do that. And, finally, that ass, Jimmy, robbed Chapiya's cake, which confirmed the break in."*

Mr Russel watched from the first floor of Evans Hall. He saw the boys beating up Jimmy and realized that he had the culprit. He did not do anything, the beating would suffice; he grinned.

"You bloody pig, you greedy dog, why did you steal Chapiya's cake? That is how he knew that someone had sneaked into his house. He did not notice the paper missing, you idiot", they screamed and beat the shit out of him. Jimmy took

the beating good heartedly. He laughed at the end. He was a tough boy. *"The cake was damn good"*, he declared. Upon which, the boys gave him another few blows.

The next day, the 9th standard students left for their home on their own. They had no booking in the Bhusaval passenger train. And there was no Jam Tin to take them to the station. Mr Davis ordered them to take a bullock cart to carry their luggage, which they did reluctantly.

The year 1972 came to an end. The students had to go home. The 11th standard students had gone home a fortnight earlier. Ganapathi had cried when he had parted with Rustom. *"Don't worry we will meet in Bombay and I will come every year for the reunion"*, assured Rustom, as he hugged the crying boy.

The students went home, happy as usual. Next year when they returned they would be the senior most students, respected by the juniors and the teachers would be expecting them to be responsible for themselves and for the juniors. Sigh! They didn't like the idea.

The Tenth Standard (1973)

Return as Senior Students

THE BHUSAVAL passenger chugged in, as usual, right on time. The first two coaches were empty. The first coach was for the Prep house boys and girls. The second coach was for the other boys. The boys helped the girls load their luggage and then loaded their own. The engine driver waited for the station master to waive the green flag. The station master, in turn, was waiting for a nod from Mr Gama and Mrs Michael, who were accompanying the students. When they confirmed all students were on board the train, the station master waved his flag. The guard blew his whistle and the train took off after blowing a long and loud whistle.

It was 5 am in the morning and VT station was teeming

with life. The cry of 'tea coffee' rent the air, as vendors started their morning rounds. Mr Gama and Mrs Michael looked harried. They had arrived the previous night and stayed overnight at their sister concern, Christ Church, in Byculla. At 4.30 am, it had not been easy to find a cab, but just when they had decided to take the local train, a cab had luckily appeared.

At the station, only a handful of students had arrived and the train would be leaving in the next half an hour. Suddenly, there was a huge flux of students and the platform was crowded. Bhusaval passenger had the usual two bogies reserved for Barnes and it filled up fast. Mr Gama was trying to check the boys against the list that he had been given by the school but to no avail. He gave up in exasperation and put away the list. He decided to check it on the train. Mrs Michael was having a relatively better experience, as the girls were standing quietly. She also could not make the Prep house boys stand at one place, so finally she instructed them, *"Just get into the train"*.

No one knew exactly if everyone had arrived, but the train started on time. Mr Gama asked Tarun Vyas, one of the seniors, to check the boys. *"I think we should wait till Thana, as many people will get in at Dadar and Thana"*, Tarun advised. Mr Gama agreed, reluctantly.

At Dadar station, a large number of students boarded the train. At Thana, however, only a few more students boarded. The Phillips twins, Rosemary and Roselin, boarded at Thana, as they lived only a station away, in Kalwa. Their brother, Brian, got into the Boys' compartment.

Mr Gama could finally check his student list; he was happy that everyone had come and that there were two more boys who were not even on the list. They had bought tickets and so he did not scold them. At Kalyan, Mrs Michael checked with him and let him know that all the girls had arrived and there was one who had bought a ticket. *"Must be Binapani Mohanty"*, said Mr Gama. *"Her brother is with you?"* she asked. *"Yes and also Ganapathi Nadar; these three got in with their own tickets"*, he confirmed.

At Igatpuri station, there was a rush to buy samosas and cutlets. "The last stop before jail", said the juniors, as they knew they would not get anything at Devlali station. The seniors did not look desperate, as they had their market permits and day permits; they could go out and buy whatever they needed.

At Devlali, the students disembarked from the train with a lot of noise. The boys offloaded their steel trunks and then helped the girls. The train guard and the station master waited for a go ahead from the Barnes' teachers. They were used to this exercise six times a year. The train stopped longer than usual but it was finally allowed to leave.

Jam Tin was waiting for them. The Prep house boys were the first to leave, followed by the girls and, finally, the junior boys and then the seniors. By then, a few seniors had already gone off to Devlali camp. They had told their friends to transfer their steel trunks. They knew Mr Gama would not count. From Devlali camp, they took a regular bus to the school Gate Lodge and walked up.

Mr Davis was standing outside his office. The senior students wished him *"Good afternoon"*, without batting an eyelid and he too did not say anything, as this was the day students came back from home. He wondered where their luggage was, but did not ask. He knew most of them were up to some mischief or the other but, today, he would overlook them.

The camp escapees entered the mess where the other train students were already eating. They took their places and ate with the rest. Nobody bothered. Tomorrow would be a different story.

The New 10th Standard Structure

This year, the 10th standard was different. Normally, there were two divisions - Sciences and Arts; but this year there was one more division - '10 ICSE', in which the students would also qualify the 10th standard. They could then join diploma courses, such as ITI, but not go to college. So those who did not plan to go to college joined this batch.

At Barnes, the decision was taken by the teachers. The best students from the 9th standard were allocated to the

Science section, the next best to the Arts section and the last batch to the 10 ICSE section. Those students who were not happy with this could approach their class teachers but no one did. The students had total faith in their teachers and knew the selection was based on merit and nothing else.

Clyde Arnold of Royal house was the head boy. His elder brother, Glenn, had also been House Captain of Royal house but he had not been the head boy. His younger brother had done better than him. Clyde had a ready smile for whoever he shouted at. He was a very good boxer and built like a bull dog. So, generally, students listened to him.

Bharat Jagoowani was the House Captain of Spence house and Bikash Chowdhury was his Vice-Captain.

The first term sports were hockey, boxing and swimming and the students plunged into them wholeheartedly. The inter-house games were as strenuous as inter-school games. There was always this pressure of getting into the school team, which was simply called the 'First Eleven'.

A Midnight Party

The Spence house senior boys decided to have a midnight party and Ganapathi was appointed as the treasurer to gather the money. The amount decided was 20 rupees from each student and it was a big headache collecting that money from most of the boys.

The seniors gave their share without a word but the

younger boys grumbled. *"You know, I get 25 rupees extra pocket money per month and you want 20 rupees?"* cribbed Babasaheb Gawli. Kailash Sawant readily gave him the money but sarcastically asked *"How much are you making?"* *"All of it is for me"*, replied the worthy, without batting an eyelid.

The House Captain and Vice-Captain also gave their share but cautioned him, *"Be careful, don't get caught and get us all into trouble"*. Bikash added, *"You know Gadre, if he finds out, he will simply cancel all our privileges this term"*.

"I am only the treasurer, the organizers are Riyaz and Christopher, please tell them", Ganapathi protested. *"You tell them"*, said the House Captain, with a dirty look. Ganapathi conveyed the message to both the organizers, but they did not bother much; all they wanted to know was how much money he had collected. It added up to 640 rupees and he put in 10 rupees to make it 650. Riyaz put in another 50 rupees, and the Arab students, Masjid, Aqeel, and Mohebi, each put in extra 100 rupees. Therefore, he had a total of 900 hundred rupees, which was a tidy sum in 1973.

They planned the menu and, after much debate, finally came to a conclusion. The Midnight Party would be organised on a Saturday night and also on a day when there was a market permit. It came a fortnight later. Riyaz, Christopher and Daniel were in-charge of purchases, while Ganapathi was in-charge of paying. They ordered *keema paratha* from Maulana. They bought two different kinds of sweets from Mathura Dairy Farm, and two crates of drinks from Empire stores. They told the owner that they would send back the empty bottles with Cyrus Irani, who was a day-scholar in Barnes. He smiled, *"What happened to your Tuck-shop man?"* he asked. *"This is for something else"*, the students giggled and Mr Irani did not ask any further questions. He knew their midnight parties were only meant for eating.

They loaded all the stuff into a cab and were on the way to school. *"If Gadre sees us in a cab, he is going to suspect something"*, said Riyaz. *"Let us get down at Candy block then"* said Christopher. *"Are you crazy? How can we carry all this stuff from Candy block and not be seen. The entire boys school will know we are having a party and someone will leak the news"*, cautioned Daniel Bardey.

After much debate, they decided to stop the cab just past Gate Lodge, where they offloaded the stuff and carried it to the swimming pool. Then, Daniel went up and brought another dozen boys with him. Between themselves, they carried all the stuff to Spence block, where they waited behind the block for the green signal. Ganapathi came down with his Mathematics note book. On getting a nod from Riyaz, he went and knocked on Mr Gadre's door. Mr Gadre said, *"I say, man! Come in, the door is open"*. Ganapathi went in and asked him about a particularly difficult Mathematics problem.

"I say, man, isn't Mishra your Mathematics teacher, why don't you go there?" he asked. Ganapathi just smiled at him. Mr Gadre thought for a while about the solution and explained it to him. *"Thank you, Sir"*, Ganapathi acknowledged, with a wide smile. It had taken them ten minutes to find the solution, during which time the boys had safely crossed the danger area. The party stuff was hidden away in a wardrobe where all the gowns and Sunday clothes hung.

The Spence house boys could not wait for lights out at 9 pm and they went to bed very happy. Mum Peron thought they were happy, as it was the weekend. Most of them tried to stay awake, but because of playing during the whole day, they had become tired. They fell asleep. Being a responsible boy, Barinder Katyal, had set his alarm for midnight and he woke with it. He quickly put the alarm off, 'Gadre has very sharp ears', he thought. He looked out of the window to see if Mr Gadre's lights were on, thankfully, they were not.

He started waking up the boys one by one and, at the same time, told them to be quiet. They lit ten candles and kept them under the beds at different places in the dormitory. There was an eerie light and shadow pattern playing on the ceiling, but the boys just wanted to have their feast. First, the snacks were distributed, followed by the main meal of *paratha* and *keema*, which the boys ate with relish. Finally, the soft drinks were distributed. After they finished, they realized that more than an hour had passed. They cleaned up the place and went to bed, happy.

The next day was a Sunday and it was a normal holiday. They had to wash their keds and whitewash them, which they did with minimum effort. On Monday morning, they informed the dormitory *hamal* that he had to get rid of the paper plates without getting caught. He was given 10 rupees for his job. The *hamal* sat on one of the culverts in front of Mr Gadre's house. After assembly, the students had gone to class and Mr Gadre was in his house. When the first period was finished, Mr Gadre headed for the 10th Science section, as he had to conduct a Physics class there. The *hamal* waited for him to enter the class. He knew he had 40 minutes to go. He went up to the Spence dormitory and took out the gunny sack from the wardrobe. Even if Gadre was in his class, the man was not going to risk taking it out from the front door. Who knew when Gadre would decide to look out of the door? Or, the Principal might suddenly appear on one of his long walks.

The *hamal* threw the gunny bag out of the back window. Mr Gadre was on the other side of the building. The *hamal* wondered who was in the 11th standard classes, which were below the dormitory. He went down to check, thankfully, no one had noticed the bag. He carried it to the swimming pool and hid it in the bushes beyond the pool. He would retrieve it in the evening and throw it out of the school campus. When the boys came upstairs in the evening to change for games, they were happy that the gunny bag was gone. They put a dozen empty soft drink bottles in a bag and gave it to Cyrus Irani, a day-scholar whose father owned Empire stores. He carried that bag every day for the next four days. No one asked him what he was carrying. Day-scholars were allowed to carry bags. On Friday, the students also gave him an empty crate to carry in the same bag. He was scared and so they had to carry it to his bus and give it to him after he had boarded. This was not easy, but the boarders managed with the help of one of their classmates' girlfriend, as the buses started from the girl's side of Evans Hall.

After the last crate went out on Monday, the boys heaved a sigh of relief. Now all signs of their party had been disposed off. Mr Gadre noticed that the Spence house boys would go into a giggling fit every time they saw him. He suspected they had been up to some mischief but he was not sure about it. Seeing his favourite, Ganapathi, he asked, *"I say, man! What is with this giggling with your dormitory mates; have they turned into girls?"* Ganapathi mumbled something and went on his way. He was not risking a reply. In the dormitory, he told the guys what the house master had said. The boys looked alarmed and their giggling immediately stopped. Soon the party was a distant memory and they settled into their studies and games.

The Easter Dance

In the 10th standard, their class teacher was their Hindi teacher, Mr Gupta; he was good to them. Their English teacher was Miss D'sa, a formidable lady. She was the house mistress of Haig-Brown, the girl's block, and a strict disciplinarian. She was also very protective of her girls.

Over the years, they had been taught English by Mr Michael, Mr Walsh, Mr Paul, and now it was Miss D'sa. Next year, it would be Mr Smith. The students agreed that Walshy had been their best English teacher, followed by Gatty. Miss D'sa was a good teacher but too strict to have fun with, unlike the others. Mr Paul was also strict but he was lenient with the 9th standard students, as he was also their class teacher. Another fun teacher was Mr Swing. He had such lovely stories to tell.

The first term was hectic and, soon, Easter was upon them. The Tuck shop man was busy selling Easter eggs and the boys complained they were too expensive. But they still bought them by sharing the cost. Thus, the eggs became more affordable.

For the boys, the best thing about Easter was the Easter Dance on the Sunday night. Monday was a holiday. For Ganapathi, it would be full of memories. Bernie was not there; she had been the one to get him on the floor during the last two years, but he still had a dozen rakhee sisters to keep him on the dance floor. It was fun but he still missed his dance teacher.

The day of the dance came and all the boys and girls from the 9th standard upward dressed up in their best. For girls, it was from the 6th standard upwards, as they were lesser in numbers. The dance started, as usual, with the head boy, Clyde Arnold, asking the head girl, Nimet Jamal, for the first dance. This multiplied with every dance. Soon, most of the boys and girls and a few teachers were on the floor.

Ganapathi chatted with Rosemary. For the first time, they were in different classes and the twins were together in 10 ICSE. *"It is okay"*, she said, when he asked her about her studies. She was very good at games. Apart from his sisters, the only other girl that Ganapathi danced with that night was Colleen Edge, who was his junior by three years. She was in Florence Nightingale and a very good looking girl.

The dance came to an end at 10.30 pm, though nobody wanted to go home. Rules were rules in Barnes and nobody flaunted it.

Mr Davis, the Principal, had been there at the beginning of the dance but he had left early, as usual.

On the next day, the boys were busy discussing the dance and how much fun they had with their favourite girl. The girls on the other hand were giggling every time the dance was mentioned. Margaret Andrews, who was in the 10th standard Arts, wondered if they could talk about boys without giggling.

Frog Hunting for Biology Lab

Ganapathi had taken Biology as his option, as against Mathematics, which was chosen by those boys who wanted to go into the engineering professional stream. At that time, he had wanted to become a doctor. The Biology lab was in Evans Hall, at the girls' side end. On the boys' side end, there was a Tuck shop and the Biology lab occupied the same space on the other side of the building.

In the Biology lab, the students had to dissect live frogs. Mr Emmanuel turned to his favourite student, Ganapathi, and asked him, *"There are a lot of frogs in the campus; why don't you catch a few for our experiment."* Ganapathi agreed. Dazed Dop (that was Mr Emmanuel's pet name) told him to keep the frogs in tin boxes after he had drilled holes in their lids. Many boys in the dormitory consumed tinned milk powder, so finding two empty tins was not a problem. They made holes in the lids, using a divider from a compass box. After lights out, they took permission from Mr Gadre and went frog-hunting, carrying two tins and a huge torch.

Ganapathi had asked his junior and friend, Surinder, for help and the younger boy had readily agreed. The idea of roaming around in the dark appealed to him. *"You think we can go to Devlali"*, he asked. *"All the shops will be shut, what's the point?"* asked Ganapathi. *"That's true"*, Surinder agreed, though with sadness. He had been thinking of a quick snack. 'Next time, we must bring some *samosas* along,' he thought. The thought of eating *samosas* with a hand that also caught frogs would be nauseating for most, but not for these boarders.

When they saw a frog, one of them would light a torch in its face. The other one would then come from behind and grab it. Soon they had filled both the tins. The next day, they went to the Biology lab and handed those tins over to the attendant. They had only one attendant for both the Chemistry and Biology labs. He always tipped them what was coming for the examinations for a price. He was a very helpful fellow.

The frogs were sedated with chloroform before they were dissected. As the boy who had brought them, Ganapathi was allowed to distribute the frogs. He always gave his favourite classmates the bigger ones.

The end of the term was nearing. Soon the examinations would be on them; students started cramming. At the same time, the intensity of the hockey matches did not come down, nor did the swimming competition. Surprisingly, this year, Spence house unseated Royal house from the swimming championship after they had won it in the last four years running.

End of the First Term

At the end of April, the boys excitedly yelled at one another. It was the last day of the school term. Boys moved their desks from Evans Hall, where they had been taken for the examinations, back to their own classrooms. The chivalrous ones helped the girls. Some of the girls helped one another, by carrying a desk between two of them. Teachers kept an eye on the students to make sure no one threw down a desk for fun; boys were capable of doing anything in Barnes.

Most students left for home by the Bhusaval passenger train, which was arranged by the school. A few of them accompanied their parents who had come to pick them up from school. Most seniors left for home on their own.

Ganapathi left with Mohanty, Kamlesh and the Katyals. Being the most responsible of the three, Barinder Katyal purchased the tickets at the railway station and also kept an eye on their luggage; the other two just roamed around even though there was no canteen there.

The Punjab Mail arrived on time and they got in after first loading their luggage. The unreserved coach was very crowded and so they got into one sleeper coach. As they were dressed in their school uniform, the TC was not angry with them. He allocated them three seats on one end of the coach and instructed them not to enter the rest of the compartment. They were very happy to get their seats and squeezed into the available space. They were five of them. The Katyals got down at Thana station, as they had to go to Bhandup. Mohanty and Kamlesh disembarked at Matunga station and Ganapathi at Khar station.

The Marathon Finals

The second term was held in the rainy season and the boys wore raincoats and gum boots. The girls also wore raincoats, with hood that looked like Red Riding's hood. The best dressed man in the monsoons was Mr Hoffman. He wore gum boots like everyone else, and a huge raincoat, along with a cap, but these things did not make him look special. What made him look special was that, after wearing a raincoat and a cap, he still carried a huge umbrella.

Football was played in the rains and cross country was also run in the rains. Only the gymnastic exercises were held in a tin shack adjacent to the study hall. In Gym, Parvez Razvi of Candy house was simply the best.

For the marathon finals, as usual, Ganapathi approached Hoffy and made sure he worked with the officials; he simply did not like to run. He was stationed at culvert number 11 where only the senior boys (over 16) would arrive. He had their second slip ready. The first was at Donkey Hill and the last one was at Gate Lodge.

The first one to reach culvert number 11 was Candy house's Surjeet Singh Kheer. He came striding up, with his long legs taking equally long strides. Then he went to sleep on the Culvert, much to the amazement of the boy and the MOD there.

Parvez Razvi was the next one to reach there, however, without breaking sweat or breathing hard. He was followed by another ten boys. Surjeet got up, shook himself and started running again. He soon caught up with the rest and overtook all of them. He was the first to finish the race and went to sleep beyond the finish line, outside Evans Hall. Parvez Razvi came in next, sweating a little but not breathing very hard. He continued to jog at one place even after finishing. He stopped that after a minute.

As expected in the gymnastic finals, Parvez bagged all the prizes in the bar events; only in the horse events, did others stand a chance.

The Third Term

The second term soon came to an end and the third term was upon them. On the prize day, Ganapathi received two prizes - one for general proficiency and the other for Science and Mathematics. His friend, Rustom, who had come with the ex-students for the annual reunion, cheered the loudest.

Two days before the Athletics day, the seniors' high jump event was being held. Eight boys started and soon four were eliminated; the remaining four made it to the finals, which were held immediately in this event. A boy was given the duty of reinstating the bar when it fell down. The teacher who conducted the event was Mr Mainguy. All the boys jumped in the usual scissors way, where they jumped over, one leg at a time, crossing them like scissors. All did this, except Parvez Razvi, who jumped over the bar in a new way; he stood next to the bar and dived over with head first, landing on the other side after a mid-air summersault.

Parvez won the event. Mr Gadre, who had finished officiating in another event, had been watching the high jump event very keenly. He then discussed his observations with Mr Russell, who was also on the field, *"I don't think what Parvez has been doing is right. There is something wrong but I don't know what it is"*. Mr Russell too was puzzled but he too did not know what was wrong. Frankly, he did not think anything was wrong. The next day, Mr Gadre came on the field with a book of Olympic rules. He showed this to Mr Mainguy, who immediately called the house captain of Candy house and Parvez. The book clearly stated that, for a high jump, the participant had to take off on one foot. However, by diving, Parvez had been taking off from both his feet, which was not permitted. It was, therefore, an illegal action.

Mr Gadre wanted to disqualify him but the Candy house captain argued that they did not know the rules and Mr Mainguy had not told them. They finally agreed to hold the event again. Parvez came in fourth.

Bharat Jagoowani and company passed out that year. Till then, the house send-off party had been a mixture of chips and drinks. This batch changed it to chicken and bread and, after that, this was routinely followed. The send-off party later became a dinner party; earlier it was a tea party.

The Eleventh Standard (1974)

The Class Teacher

IN JANUARY 1974, the first day of the school was something new for Ganapathi and his classmates. They observed the junior boys and thought back over the years. This was their final year and they realized they would be sad when they would leave at the end of the year. So, they decided to enjoy every minute of it.

Their class teacher was the genius mathematician, Mr Mishra, who was also completely absent minded. He had a fantastic smile; a truly handsome man. Sometimes, he came to the class with his tie undone, his buttons undone and uncombed hair. As the class teacher, he had to approve their purchases for class work. Ganapathi once gave him a voucher with a request for half a brown paper. He signed that too. His favourite student was Barinder Katyal, who had taken additional Mathematics and was also the house captain of Spence house.

Students used to love it when Mr Mishra was the MOD, because they could do as they pleased. He seldom noticed anything apart from his Mathematics. The 11th standard science students loved him. Whenever they needed anything, he always okayed that. Other teachers watched with amusement when he walked in the rain without an umbrella but everybody acknowledged the fact that he was a genius par excellence.

Mr Gadre taught Physics and the quiet Mr Emmanuel, taught both Chemistry and Biology. They had a large bodied Mr D A Smith as their English teacher; with him there was never a dull moment. He had joined Barnes the previous year. He always told them that his wife was on the way in a truck.

Mr Smith was an ordained priest and a bachelor. He was the only teacher who came to school and told the students that his pet name in his previous school was Gatty. Normally, it was the students who came up with pet names, such as Chapiya and Tatoori.

The 11th standard students were also a privileged lot. Teachers did not normally shout at them to study. They were supposed to be old enough to know that. Most of them had earlier been either prefects or Captains of their houses, which added to their responsibility.

While the head girl, Smita Vassa, was in 11th standard Science; the head boy, Ravinder Singh, was in 11th standard Arts.

Swimming Certificate for Completion

Ganapathi had decided that he had to top the class, so he started studying hard from day one. After lights were out at 9 pm, he would continue to study on the staircase landing till about 11.30 pm every night and also woke up at 5.30 am every morning. He would be back at his books by 6 am. He slept at 11.30 pm because his house master, Mr Gadre, had told him that half an hour sleep before midnight was equal to two hours of sleep after midnight.

The first term sports were hockey, swimming and boxing, and the junior classes went ahead with the sports. Ganapathi, by virtue of being in the 11th standard, was in the B team of all games, as his classmate, Barinder, felt it would be embarrassing to put him in the C or D teams, which were full of the boys from the junior classes.

For swimming, Ganapathi decided that he would participate only in the 200 m events, as he could not swim fast. Swimming was dominated by Jimmy Parvaresh, the Royal house captain, but Spence house had more good swimmers and they won the cup.

The 200 m finals were held without heats, as there were very few participants. All others had finished the race but Ganapathi had still to complete three lengths. Egged on by his house, he completed it. There was also a clamour for giving him a certificate for completion. Mr Davis frowned and the students came running back.

Gatty's English class was fun, as he had a habit of enacting his stories. But when he got angry, his face would become red and he would shout, which would scare most of the students. But he would also cool down fast.

The 11th standard Arts and Sciences classes were conducted next door to each other in Spence house block. The students knew one another, as they had all been together in the lower classes. The '10 ICSE' class was conducted in block '5'.

The 10th standard Arts classes were also conducted in the Spence house block. Vishaka Saranjame was a favourite with Ganapathi, because she had her nose like the then Prime Minister, Indira Gandhi. She was in his sister house, Florence Nightingale, and they would team up for the debating cup later in the year along with Erica D'eabro and Barinder Katyal.

Unequal Boxing Fights

The boxing rounds started. The good one sailed through the initial rounds easily. Ganapathi was amazed to reach the quarter finals after winning the first three rounds. In the quarter finals, he was up against his classmate from Greaves house, Ravinandan Mohanty, whose sister, Bina Mohanty, was a very good athlete.

Mr Gadre was the referee inside the ring. He was surprised to see a Nadar versus Mohanty bout and knew it was lopsided. The bell rang and Ganapathi advanced. He got a socker on his face and when he hit back, Mohanty had disappeared. He turned to his left and saw Mohanty. He was again floored by a socker and when he wanted to hit back, Mohanty had vanished. What he did not see was that, after hitting him hard, Mohanty would move to his left. Mr Gadre stopped the fight and announced, *"Unequal fight- Blue wins"*. Mohanty helped Ganapathi out of the ring, as he was bleeding profusely from his nose. Attendants put ice on it and made him sit with his face up. Mr Gadre gave Mr Gama an earful for making such pairs.

"They weigh the same and have to box with those who weigh the same, it's the way we pair them. Now if Mohanty is good, what am I supposed to do?" Mr Gama clarified to Mr Gadre.

Gadre was not happy till Gama reminded him that, *"Nadar had reached the quarter finals after defeating three students on the way; he is not a novice, though I agree that he is no match for Mohanty"*. Mr Gadre had to accept the argument though he still felt that it was a lopsided bout.

Mohanty apologized to Ganapathi, while their classmate,

a mutual friend, Kamlesh Jagoowani, said, *"You can't fight like a man. Why were you moving away so slyly?"*. *"That's how you box, you moron"* replied Mohanty. Ganapathi told him that he was okay and a visibly embarrassed Mohanty went back to his house mates. He wasn't happy to beat up his fellow classmate who was more of a scholar and less of a boxer. *"How the hell did he reach the quarter finals?"* he asked his housemate, Myron.

"The judges must have considered his class marks, he is brilliant", said the worthy with a laugh. *"You won, now drop it"*, he concluded.

In Hockey, Ganapathi was in the house B team by virtue of being in the 11th standard. Barinder Katyal, his Captain, had decided at the beginning of the year itself that he would put his classmate in the B team for all games, only as a mark of respect to his final year but not for his ability at games, which was dismal.

One day, while walking to the dining hall, Surinder Katyal tripped and fell. He had been tripped by Ganapathi by mistake. Katyal hurt himself and was furious. *"Can't you see where you are going; what do you wear glasses for?"* he demanded. Surinder was his junior. *"What are you going to do about it?"* Ganapathi asked pleasantly. Upon this, Surinder landed a square punch on his jaw, taking him by surprise. Ganapathi recovered to hit him back. Soon, it was a free for all fight.

Barinder, who came from behind, was shocked, as both of them were very good friends. He stopped them and shouted at his younger brother. *"Surinder, how dare you raise your hand on a senior?"* *"He tripped me"* Surinder replied. *"It was a mistake"*, Ganapathi tried to clarify. *"Stop fighting and go to the mess"*, shouted Barinder. They both did not argue, as he was, after all, their house captain. After the meal, Surinder came and apologized to Ganapathi; they hugged and kissed, and all was well.

The 11th standard students started studying hard, even though this was only their first term. They knew their marks would decide the college that they would get into. Higher marks meant admission to a good college and those students who had really high marks could skip the first year at the college and go straight to the second year. That was the level of respect that ISCE Senior Cambridge commanded.

The boxing finals had the Colonel from the Artillery Centre as the Chief Guest. In his speech, he told them how they could join the army and also why they should join the army. *"It will be like a continuation of your boarding school"*, he concluded. The boys were impressed and so were some of the girls.

The Last Easter Ball

Soon it was time for the Easter Ball and the students grew excited. They all dressed up in their best attire and were very careful while having dinner. They did not want stains on their best dance dress. Many students wore expensive cufflinks and perfumes.

The girls looked dainty and very different from their daily looks, where most behaved like tom boys. On this night, however, they looked and talked like ladies. One had to bow down to them while asking for a dance. They were supposed to show some courtesy before agreeing, but most just started giggling.

It was fun and started with the head boy, Ravinder Singh, asking the head girl, Smita Vassa, for a dance. Soon everyone was on the dance floor; some people pushed one another, sometimes by mistake, but sometimes deliberately. Good behaviour had its limits. This was, after all, a boarding school.

The dance ended at 10.30 pm as usual, however, the romantics were reluctant to leave the dance floor. The rest trooped out, shouting out byes to the girls.

Broken Spectacles

The examinations were upon them and the ritual of carrying their desks to Evans Hall started in earnest one afternoon after lunch. The boys, as usual, helped the girls. Some girls, working in pairs, carried their desks themselves. Obviously, they did not want any help from the boys.

Examinations were a serious affair, but because it was the

first term, some students were seen fooling around, as they did through the rest of the term.

One day, while Ganapathi was studying something, a friend from the junior section in the dormitory, Iqbal, asked him if he would like to go to the Tuck shop. Ganapathi did not reply, as he did not hear him. He was concentrating on his book. Iqbal threw a pillow at him, which dislodged and broke his pair of glasses. A fist fight broke out between the two friends. They were pulled apart by other boarders, who also chided them, *"You are friends, why are you behaving like jungles?"*

After a few hours, both apologized to each other and hugged, which brought relief to the other boarders, who were upset that friends, particularly the seniors, had a fight. Iqbal offered to pay for the glasses. *"Never mind, I am happy. I am going to tell Gadre that I cannot see anything without my glasses and so will not attend school tomorrow. I will go and get another pair. I will see two movies while you great men will be attending classes"* Ganapathi gloated. Iqbal smiled back; he was happy that it had ended well.

Mr Gadre agreed to let Ganapathi go and gave him a chit to give to the MOD before he left. Next day, he took a bus to Nasik. He first ordered a pair of glasses, and then went and saw two movies. He had to sit in the first row at the cinema, as he could not see the screen otherwise. Later, he had lunch at Haghigihi's restaurant. Ali Akbar was at the cash counter and did not charge him. That made him doubly happy.

In the evening, he went back with his new pair of glasses. *"Let me know when you want to go back to Nasik"*, said Iqbal cheekily. Ganapathi laughed along with the others.

The term ended and it was time to go home. Ganapathi went to meet Mr Hoffman. He liked to meet his old house master, who was still his Scout Master. *"Nadar, you are not leaving today?"* Mr Hoffman enquired. *"Of course, I am going! I just came to say bye to you"*. *"Come on in"* Mr Hoffman offered him cake and tea, and they chatted for a while.

Mr Hoffman said he was going to spend the holidays in the school. *"How will you pass the time?"* asked his favorite student. *"There are wards of the school who may stay back. I will take care of them and they will keep me busy, you don't worry"*, he smiled at the thoughtful boy.

Ganapathi did not go with the Bhusaval passenger school trip. He left with his own friends; they had called for a cab from Devlali. Times had changed.

The New Scout Leader

It was the first Scout meeting in the second term. The Scout leader, Deepak Vassa, who was in the 10th standard, had not come for the meeting. He had not attended the last two meetings in the first term. Hoffy knew he had to take a decision, as he knew all the Scouts knew the rules and expected him, above all, to uphold them.

He looked around the serious faces and was happy.

"I am glad to see all the familiar faces and also the new ones who joined us in the first term.

Number one, you all know that if someone does not attend three meetings, he will be out of the Scouts, unless he is ill or informs me of the reason of his non-attendance.

Number two, our Scout leader has not attended three consecutive meetings and he has not informed me the reason. So, I think he does not want to be in the Scouts.

Number three, we have to appoint a new Scout leader after making sure he is fit to lead the Scouts.

Number four, Nadir has been with us now for six years, since he joined Barnes and was in my Block. He is a disciplined boy and also very good in studies. He has never missed a single Scout session. The only problem is, sometimes, he gets very angry and that will not do for a leader. He has to control his anger and only then can he control his troops.

I now appoint Ganapathi Nadar of the Eagles troop as the Scout leader. He will now say a few words" Hoffy concluded.

A beaming Nadar stepped forward from his place at the head of the Eagles to stand beside the Scout Master as the head of the Scouts. *"Thank you"*, was all that he said.

Later in the day, he met Deepak Vassa and asked him why he had not attended the Scout meeting. *"It was nice in the junior classes but now I am not so much interested, so I never came"*, he said, with a smile. Deepak was a quiet boy.

His sister was Ganapathi's classmate and also the head girl of the school.

When he was made the Scout leader, Ganapathi did not realize what it meant and he would not know that until the month of August.

Sports in the Second Term

Being the second term, it was football where the good players played their hearts out while the slackers stood somewhere and passed the time. The cross country run and gym practices were also going on at full swing.

That evening, it was the cross country run for Spence house. Barinder Katyal had separated them into age groups of Novice, Junior, Inter and Seniors. He sent the Novices forward and then the Juniors, followed by the Inters. When it was the turn of the Seniors, Ganapathi said, *"I will be part of the officials, so I don't think I need to practice".* *"I don't care if you are going to become the Principal of the school, you will practice with the others and now you run with me",* ordered Barinder.

Ganapathi was ready with a retort when he observed his house captain was really angry; so he kept quiet. He ran with the others till Donkey Hill and then started walking. Barinder ignored him and continued running. He knew that Nadar would run after some time. He was also confident that he would not take a short cut but will complete the course.

Despite his faults and a dislike for sports, he considered Ganapathi as an honest boy and, therefore, expected him to complete the course.

As expected, Ganapathi arrived 20 minutes after the last man. He looked upset but Katyal ignored him. His younger brother, Surinder Katyal, who was a friend of Nadar, said, *"You completed the course, congratulations! I will buy you one samosa as your reward"*. Ganapathi started laughing and the tension passed.

Christopher Phillips was in the 10th standard. Spence house boys were thrilled when he was appointed the captain of the school football team. Chris was a short boy, but what he lacked in height, he made up in speed. He could sprint from one end of the field to the other in double quick time which, at most times, left his opponents in disarray. He also had very good control of the ball.

Debating Cup Victory

Then the debating season started. Barinder spoke to Nadar, *"You are the only one in the team who has the experience of debating last year. We expect you to win us the cup. It is the only cup that you can win us. You are not good at anything else."* *"I will also win the Elocution and the study cup"*, he replied, while not at all bothered to be told that he was not good at anything else. The truth was accepted. That is what you learnt at Barnes.

Ganapathi had been part of the debating since the previous year but he had actually started participating from the floor two years before that. He was the most experienced debater not only in the Spence house but also in the school. It was a joint team from the Spence and Nights houses.

The team members were Ganapathi and Barinder from Spence House; and Erica D'abreo, the house captain, and Vishaka Saranjame of Nights. They were a formidable team and other teams knew that.

In the first debate, Ganapathi was declared as the best speaker. In the second debate, Erica was declared as the best speaker. In the third, they were both declared as the joint first. They won the cup easily. Erica was declared the best debater of the school. Nadar was disappointed, but what consoled him was that he had lost to his own house girl.

If it was his experience that won Spence and Nights the cup that year, in 1975, they won it based on a combined experience of both Erica and Vishaka. The house vice-captain, Kareem Merchant said, *"We won because we clapped the loudest; the other houses did not cheer properly"*, he looked at Ganapathi, with a mischievous twinkle on his face. Knowing that he was being bated, Nadar ignored him.

Flag Hoisting Honour

A fortnight before the Independence Day, Hoffy spoke at a Scout meeting, *"We will be right at the front. All of you make sure your dress is spic and span, and your keds are sparkling white. Ganapathi, you will be hoisting the National flag and, now, I will train you for it."* Ganapathi almost fainted with happiness. It would be his highest honour in his school life. In his mind he thought, *'Thank you, Deepak'.*

"First you march ahead six steps, and then turn right and march ten steps. You hold both the ropes and pull the rope that is rolled around the flag. You can look up and check which one is the right one", said Hoffy.

"Can we do it with a flag?" Ganapathi asked.

"Yes, we will before the assembly on that day, you don't worry", assured Hoffy.

It was the 15th of August 1974 and Nadar was excited. After breakfast, he went up to Evans Hall and assembled the Scouts who were roaming around the hall, checking out the boards. *"There is no board for Scouts",* one of them said. *"I doubt we will ever have a board"* said another.

"Why don't you all assemble in your own troops?" asked the Scout leader loudly. Once they had fallen into a formation, he checked their uniforms, lapels, keds and ropes. Hoffy walked in and also inspected them one at a time. He did not want any untidiness. He knew that the Principal was very capable of pointing it out in the assembly if he noticed any tardiness. After getting satisfied, he started tying the flag up and sent it up. He then made Ganapathi march up, as taught, and made him pull the rope.

The flag opened on cue. *"We should have a fan to blow on it so that it flutters"*, suggested one young Scout. Hoffy glared at him, *"No talking in the ranks"*. Silence descended.

They repeated the exercise thrice. Both Hoffy and Nadar were satisfied. Now, Hoffy tied the flag up with some rose petals inside. The assembly hall started filling in noisily. Ravinder Singh shouted, *"Silence"*, and it became a little less noisy. Some boys would stop talking only if and when they saw the Principal.

The students were all in and then the teachers came in. Today, they wore their gowns with colours. The more degrees they had, the more coloured stripes their gowns had. The Principal, Mr J L Davis, was the last to enter. He took his place at the podium and looked at Mr Hoffman, who was also dressed in his Scout uniform.

"Troop leader, step forward and hoist the flag", he said quietly. His voice travelled right through the silent hall. Ganapathi did not hesitate. He stepped forward, unfurled the flag and saluted smartly. On cue, the students started singing the National Anthem, with Mr C Paul at the piano. The Anthem ended and Ganapathi went back to his place at the head of his troops. Hoffy was right at the back. He gave his troop leader a 'well done' smile. Nadar glowed. He hoped the photographer had taken a good picture. Luckily, he did have one, which was used in the year's *Barnicle*.

After that, they sang a hymn, followed by their daily

prayer. Mr Davis gave a small speech on the freedom struggle and told the students they should value their freedom, which had been obtained after a struggle that had lasted a hundred years. *'Ninety actually'*, thought some of the students but they kept quiet.

After assembly, Hoffy had some snacks for his troops, which they ate in a manner that belied the fact that they had breakfast just before the assembly. The rest of the day was a holiday and so they went off to play. No play for Ganapathi; he took out his books and sat on the landing. Mr Gadre, who had come up to meet the Matron, smiled at him and said, *"Nice to see you hoisting the flag, you deserve the honour; you are the most hard working student that I have seen in my time"*. Ganapathi could not stop glowing for the next few hours.

On the day of the cross country run, as predicted, Ganapathi was part of the officials, thanks to Hoffy always choosing him as his assistant. The finals went off well and the boys were happy. Girls did not have cross country run at Barnes.

Fun during the Michaelmas Holidays

The second term ended and the Michaelmas holidays arrived, which were only for nine days. Ganapathi decided to stay back. Most students went home and there were about 25 boys who stayed back; they moved into one dormitory.

They had lots of fun, as there were special games for them

every day and the prizes always comprised food stuff. They also had a dance, which was more fun with less people. As the teachers had stayed back, there were more teachers on the dance floor than the students.

A Bagful of Prizes

The third term started after the holidays. The 11th standard students were both nervous and sad at the same time, *"The last term at Barnes! They could not believe they had hated the school while in the junior block and had always said that it was a jail where you had to pay to stay and, thus, making it worse than a regular jail where one did not have to pay".*

Teachers stopped scolding the 11th standard students and also the 10th ICSE students. They could be late for meals, classes and assembly and no one said anything. They were nervous about their public examinations and did not want to add to their tension.

Athletics, swimming and cricket kept the students busy along with their study. Surprisingly, Spence house won the swimming cup; Royal had been winning it for so many years in the past continuously. Christopher Phillips won many prizes in athletics. Spence house went on to win the Hodge, which meant they became the school champions. Barinder Katyal was on top of the world, as he was the Captain of Spence house.

Reunion came and Ganapathi was pleased to see Rustom

again. *"This year, I am getting five prizes, including that of the best student of Barnes"* he said proudly. Rustom patted him on the back. On the prize day, they were all dressed in full white with ties. Ganapathi forgot to button up his shirt sleeves and his sleeves flapped all the five times he went up to the dais to receive his prizes, which included the Kennelly medal for the 'student of the year'.

Next morning, at assembly, Mr Davis sent a broad message to the students, *"Normally, no one bothers how you dress but when you come up to receive a prize, everyone is looking at you. So, if your sleeves are flapping, as if you are going to take off like a bird, it reflects badly on you and your teachers. Outside guests were present there, the ex-students were present there and you are the prize winner and you don't know how to dress?"*

Ganapathi almost died of shame and thanked his stars that Mr Davis was sweet enough not to name him. Mr Davis did not name him because, normally, he was not a tardy dresser and that he was extremely well behaved. Also, perhaps, because he was the best student of the school and he did not want to insult him. Ganapathi confided with his friends that Mr Davis had been talking about him. *"We know"*, was the chorus. He fled to sulk by himself before going to class. Once he opened his books, he had forgotten about the scolding and started solving sums for Mr Mishra.

For athletics, Ganapathi decided to take part in the 1500 m event only, as he could not run fast.

Frequent Headaches

Ganapathi was frequently suffering from headaches. He did not know if it was because of his continued studying long hours or due to any other reason. He knew if his glass number changed, then his head always ached. It was a Saturday and he told the MOD, Mr Emmanuel, that he wanted to go to Nasik to get his eyes tested.

"I cannot give you permission, you will have to ask the Principal", said Mr Emmanuel. So, Nadar went to the Principal's office, but he was not there. The attendant told him that Mr Davis was in his home on the first floor. Ganapathi waited in the lawn while the attendant informed the Principal.

Mr Davis appeared at the window on the first floor, dressed in a night gown. He listened to the student and suspected that he was looking for a free day permit. *"Get lost!"* he said sternly. Ganapathi was shocked. Mr Davis had gone inside. Ganapathi was confused and wondered he had been a serious student; so why did the Princy think he was fooling around?

Ganapathi was very upset. *'He wants me to get lost, Oh! Yes, I will'*, he thought and went walking down the Hill. He caught a bus and went to Nasik to see the doctor. His eyesight had worsened and he had to change his glasses. The doctor gave him a prescription and the optician said he had to come back after a couple of hours.

To pass time, Ganapathi went to Haghighi's hotel, where he was told by Ali Akbar that some Barnes' boys were staying at the hotel. He went upstairs to find his dormitory mates, Majid and Akeel Badri, in a hotel room. They listened to his tale in amazement and could not believe that a serious student like Nadar had just walked out of school without taking permission. They ordered a *chicken biriyani* for him, followed by an ice cream. The Middle Eastern students were rich and also generous to their friends. Ganapathi sat and talked with them till 5 pm and then left for the optician. *"You come back here if Davis throws you out"*, said Akeel. Ganapathi smiled back. He did not expect to be thrown out, as his glasses had really changed. His reason for defiance had become valid.

He collected his glasses and caught the bus back to the school. Instead of walking past the Principal's office, he walked past the hospital. It was a wise precaution. If he had met Mr Davis on the way in, he would probably have been caned. He was in time for dinner. He showed Mr Emmanuel his new pair of glasses. Mr Emmanuel asked him if he had met Mr Davis and he told him that he had, truthfully.

After dinner, he went to his dormitory. He felt guilty, as he normally did not break rules like he had done earlier that day. He went down to his house master and told him all that had happened. Mr Gadre listened to him calmly and was satisfied when he found out that his glasses number had indeed changed for the worse. *"It is okay, Nadar, but please do not make this a habit. You should have come to me. I could have given you permission; you did not have to go to the Principal".*

A Mile Run

While the other Spence house boys practiced the other sporting events, Nadar practiced only the mile run. He would wake up at 6 am every morning and then go down to the athletics field, with Mr Gadre's permission, and run the mile. This went on for two months.

On the day of the finals, he was the first to take off at the start. Much to the shock of the whole school, he led in the first round, after 300 m. A loud cheer went up for the unusual and unexpected leader. At the end of the second round, at 700 m, he was still leading and the cheers increased. In the third round, the regular athletes started increasing their pace and Nadar was soon lost somewhere in the middle. He tried his best but could not keep up. In the final round, he was in the last ten and very disappointed. After the race, he sat under a tree all by himself and looked like he was about to start crying. Mr Russell, who was on the field, came up to him.

"Nadar, what is the problem? You surprised all of us by leading the first two rounds and setting the pace for the others", Mr Russell said, with a gentle smile.

"*But I could not keep it up; I had been practicing it for the last two months*", Nadar replied.

"*When did you practice?*" asked Chapiya.

"*At 6 am in the morning everyday*", said Nadar with pride.

"*At what time was the final held?*" asked the master. "*At 3 pm*", the student replied.

"*Exactly, that is the problem; you practiced at 6 am when it is nice and cold. The race was held at 3 pm in the afternoon sun. You are bound to get tired, as you are not used to the heat. You should have practiced in the lunch break, you would have been better placed today. It is not your fault. Come on, cheer up! You are the Kennelly medalist for 'the best student of the year'; you cannot be the best miler too*", Chapiya laughed and Nadar smiled. His bad mood vanished with the teacher's explanation.

Outgoing Students Play for Teachers

As a school tradition, the school leavers had to organise a play for the teachers before leaving the school. One of the day-scholars proposed a play that he had heard on the radio. Ganapathi added a few characters to it and the play was ready. Its theme was a job interview. In the play, characters gave bizarre replies and, thus, no one initially gets the job. In the end, a person got the job because his father happened to be the MP of that area. And he got it even after he slapped the interviewer by mistake in the process of waving his arms.

The interviewer for this play was the serious student, Barinder Katyal. He did his job so well that Mrs Tess Davis was very impressed and chose him to play the role of a police inspector in her play. Every year, Mrs Davis organised a play on one of the books by Agatha Christie. The plays were always a hit, as she was a fantastic director.

The Final Examinations

After the athletics and dance events were over, the ex-students left. Now, only the final examinations were left.

Nadar wrote to his father for an extra 150 rupees for the farewell feast. The money arrived the next week and he gave it to his house captain, Katyal.

It was the Biology practical final examination. As expected, the lab attendant tipped the students that a cockroach was to be dissected during the examination on that day. Students pulled out their books and started looking at it with great interest. Others crowded around Ganapathi and other good students, and made them repeat what had to be done.

"First draw the image and then start the dissection", was a general advice to all. So the students started looking hard at the drawings. They had to show the alimentary system of the cockroach. The external examiner was shocked to see all the students first drawing the alimentary system

without even touching the cockroach. She thought it might have been the teacher's advice not knowing that it was a student's word. So everyone scored full marks for their drawing. For the dissection, their marks depended on their (gentle) skills. Ganapathi scored zero in dissection, as he broke the cockroach. He went on to do well in the later papers and was expected to top the class.

Special Prize for Debating

It was the last assembly for the 11th standard students and the 10 ICSE students. Mr Davis wished them well after the hymns and prayers. The prizes for the third term games were given. Spence and Florence Nightingale got a shield for winning the debating cup. They also got another shield for studies. Erica D'abreo received a certificate for the best debater of the school.

Ganapathi received a certificate for the best debater among the boys. This particular prize had never been given in the past at Barnes. As a special consideration that year, it was awarded to Ganapathi. In his heart, he thanked Mr Swing, who was their house mentor and also in-charge of debating and, thus, in a position to award him an extra certificate. He had recommended to Mr Davis that Nadar deserved it, as he was only half a point behind the leader. Mr Davis had agreed, because he knew Nadar was a good student and an enthusiastic debater.

The Student Party

The day of the party dawned and everyone was excited. The 11th standard students went to Devlali, hired cycles and bought 30 chickens from a nearby farm. Mrs Swing, who was their house mentor's wife, told them that 15 chickens were spoilt. So, they went back to the farmer. There was no need to fight, as he changed the chicken for them.

Mrs Swing was a very good cook and the dinner was excellent. When Mr and Mrs Swing came to meet the boarders during the dinner party, they got a noisy three cheers.

After eating to their fill, the junior students gave presents to their seniors. Ganapathi received a very expensive shaving set and, interestingly, he had not even started shaving.

There were two more weeks for the term to end.

The 11th standard and 10 ICSE students left for their homes the day after the term ended. Their luggage was loaded on a bullock cart, which carried it to the station.

The boys walked down to catch a bus to the station. On the way down the Hill, they turned back for taking one more glance at the school on the Hill but they could not see their school. Their eyes were clouded with tears.

The Reunion (39 Years Later)

On Way to Barnes

THIRTY NINE years later, thanks to Facebook, a lot of Barnicles had started coming for the yearly reunion. Earlier, we had one dormitory for the ex-students and now we needed three.

Akbar was 15 years younger than Ganapathi but that did not stop the senior from calling him and asking, *"How are you going to Barnes?"*

"I am driving, Sir; you want to come along?" asked Akbar.

"Yes! That is why I called", Ganapathi said.

"I will be leaving around noon from Mira Road; you please come there by 11.30 am", requested Akbar.

Ganapathi was very excited; he was going back to his

old school after 39 years and his heart was full of joy. He reached Mira Road at 11 am, as he was very keen and eager to reach his school quickly and, therefore, in a hurry. He called Akbar to inform him that he had reached the meeting spot. Akbar was on his way; he landed up 15 minutes later. Ganapathi was having tea at that time. He asked his friend if he would also like to take a cup of tea, which Akbar refused, *"I don't like tea at odd hours".*

"Can we leave?" Akbar asked.

"No! We have to wait for Yogesh Naik; he is on his way. I tried calling him but he did not pick up his phone. He must be in the local train; we will wait", Ganapathi replied.

Half an hour later, Yogesh turned up and they hugged one another. Yogesh was pleased to see Nadar and commented, *"You look the same, I mean your face and colour, size you are too fat!"* Nadar did not bother to reply. Akbar got into the driver's seat and Ganapathi sat by his side. Yogesh sat at the back of the car and lit a cigarette.

They took the road to Thane and were soon on the Mumbai-Nasik highway. *"I am feeling hungry"*, said Ganapathi, and added, *"Wait! We are meeting one more guy from Barnes on the way and then we will eat. He is my class mate and I have not seen him in 20 years!"*

The said classmate was waiting on the highway, where he had caught up with another Barnicle. Islam ul-Haq was a very eloquent and convincing speaker. He had a small ponytail to add to his charm and was very witty. Soon they were laughing like children.

They stopped to have lunch and were soon on their way. They did not go to Nasik, but instead took a turn at Gooty. There is a small road that goes via Levit and South Devlali, and then straight to Barnes, without even touching Devlali proper. After a while, they stopped again, this time for tea.

At the tea shop, they also fed a dog, happily. It was a lovely shop, overlooking a lake, which had a little water in it.

When they reached Barnes, they decided to go to Devlali to buy some things, like drinks and cigarettes, which would not be available at the school. At Barnes, the rule for the ex-students is that one can smoke and drink but only in the dormitory. Outside the dormitory, one has to behave appropriately in front of the students.

The New Barnes

At the gate, they met the security and paid 2,250 rupees for their 3-day stay. Then, they went to the dormitory, which was their own, the one they had stayed in when they were students at the school. The buildings that they had stayed in were no longer in use. They had been swept clean only for their use for these three days of the reunion. The management had declared them unsafe for the current students. As they are heritage buildings, they cannot be demolished. The boys' new dormitories were now on one side of Candy and Spence blocks. Likewise, the girls' dormitories and small boys were housed by the side of Haig-Brown.

Next to Evans Hall was a new Coles building and behind it were all the classes in one massive structure. In front of Evans Hall, there was a stage on which the boxing finals used to take place. Now, it had a discarded MIG-21 fighter plane for display, presented by an ex-student, Air Marshall Tipnis. Behind Lloyd block, there was a Patton tank for display, gifted by another former student. Near the tank was a church, which did not exist during their time. Those days, on one end of Evans Hall first floor, there was a church for both Protestants and the Catholics.

The old three swimming pools were now in ruins. A brand new and sparkling Olympic size swimming pool had been built near the sports ground where, in the past, the B team football and cricket matches used to be played. That is on the other side of athletics field. The shed between the two fields was still there.

Earlier, there used to be one mess for everyone. Now there was a boys' mess and a girls' mess. It was actually the same mess hall; they had only built a wall in between. The food was much better now.

Gate Lodge looked exactly the same. They were housed in Spence block and Ganapathi stared at the Master's home on the ground floor, expecting Mr Gadre to come out and say, *"I say, man! You are late"*. But, he was now in Devlali; Ganapathi planned to meet him the next day.

Meeting Old Mates

On the first floor, the first person that Ganapathi met was Munnu Hussain. He had first come back to the school as an ex-student 40 years ago and, surprisingly, he was still coming back, Munnu greeted him and they introduced themselves to this bunch of veterans in the reunion. Christopher Phillips walked in and Ganapathi hugged him like a long lost brother. There were tears in his eyes, as he kissed his dormitory mate on both his cheeks. Kaisar Hakeem on the next bed said, *"I remember you"*. *"Yeah, very few students had my skin colour in those days"*, Ganapathi replied and they all laughed. It was good to be back at Barnes.

Close to midnight, Rustom Parvaresh his childhood hero and mentor, turned up. Ganapathi hugged him for as long as he could. Along came the tall Anil Puri and the even taller Ruallah Naimi. Michael Bardey was also in this group with Shapoor Izadiyar.

Shapoor immediately went to Munnu Hussain's bed and sprang on him. The sleepy Munnu woke up with, *"You damn Iranians, why don't you go back to Iran?"*. Michael Bardey chatted with Christopher and Ganapathi, and all other Spence house boys. It was very late in the night before they all fell asleep.

It was Thursday; they would be here till Sunday. Dinner had been delivered to the dormitory, so that late arrivals had something to eat.

The next morning, Ganapathi rose at 5 am to bathe and dress up. He still had an aversion to bathing naked in a group. At 6 am, Rustom, Munnu, Colin Massey, Kaisar Hakeem and Shetty set out for a walk. They continued their morning walk on Friday, Saturday and Sunday.

On the fields, they could see Ruallah Naimi, with his camera, and Shreeprakash Ghanekar roaming around. They waved out to them and kept walking. They went downhill, past Gate Lodge and all the way to the nearest village, Bagur, where they stopped to have tea at the bus stop. Ganapathi purchased all the English papers available. He then took an auto to go back. *"Coming is downhill but return is uphill; I am not going to walk"*, he declared. Kaisar Hakeem came with him, while the rest walked back.

After the students finished their breakfast, it was the turn of the Alumni. They were surprised to see the bright chairs and the clean tables, sparkling. Eggs, bread, porridge, tea, coffee was all there for them. There were even fans. The dormitory also had three fans, which was unknown during their time.

After tasting the porridge, which they declared was as bad as in the past; they went on to devour the bread and eggs with lots of jam and butter. Those days in the past it was margarine. Mr Thakoor, in the mess, really looked after them very well. And the smiling Mr Mathew was always open to suggestions.

Denise Tully was one of the students who came here every reunion. She was a niece of their famous Mum Tully. Their favourite Mum Peron's daughter was the school nurse now and she was as sweet as her mother.

Ganapathi was delighted to see Brian Phillips. Brian hugged him with obvious delight, and said *"I am in the merchant navy and my wife is a teacher here. She wants to meet you because you are an author and journalist".*

They went down to the cricket field where there was a match being played between the past and the present students. The Alumni chose the youngest amongst themselves to face the current students. The students played very well and though the Alumni tried hard, they could not come anywhere near the current students. Ganapathi, Munnu and Christopher had fun as the commentators.

Then lunch, which was far better than anything they had eaten at Barnes in the past, was served, but they did not compare. They were just happy to be back. After lunch, the seniors went off to sleep, while the younger lot, after waiting for the mandatory hour gap, went swimming. *"The water is very cold"*, was their only comment when they came back later.

The evening tea had not changed. It was still bun, butter and a banana, but nobody complained. Christopher, Kaisar and Ganapathi sat at the flag pole for old times' sake and viewed Broken Tooth that had not changed a bit.

They went down to check the blind well, but it was not there. Weeds had overgrown it and time had filled it. They went to check the quarries, which were still there but shallower than before.

The Social

After dinner was the social for the Alumni and the current students. Ganapathi's classmates, Barinder Katyal and Manoj Suri, turned up, as promised, in Suri's car. They were greeted with warmth by the Barnicles of the Seventies. Both had a bath, as they wanted to be fresh for the dance. After dinner, they went to the first floor of Evans Hall. The students who had dinner half an hour before them were already dancing in groups.

Initially, the boys danced with the boys and the girls danced with the girls. Munnu Hussain walked in and stopped the music. He then took over as MC and announced, *"Please, may I have the head boy on the floor. Now go and ask the head girl for a dance, start the music"*. After a while, the music stopped and Munnu told them to go and pick new partners. In a few minutes, the dance floor was full of swaying young and old students and a few teachers.

Ganapathi danced once, with his adopted child, Hemu, before she ran off with her friends.

Shireen was asking Pam to dance with her. Ganapathi, who was sitting nearby, asked her to dance with the boys. *"None of the boys is getting up"*, she said. *"I will dance with you"*, he said, as he got up. However, after one dance, he came back and sat down. As he felt like smoking, he walked out of the hall and went to the side of Evans Hall, so that no staff saw him. Michael Bardey, his old house captain and a football star, was already there. They smoked together and reminisced about the old times. They talked about his mischievous brother, Daniel, who had passed away. Both were silent for a few minutes, as they thought of Daniel and his ready smile and his umpteen mischievous ideas.

"You know, he fell off the second floor at Barnes, while he was crossing over during a night, and survived that fall. But he could not survive a small illness", said Michael, with deep sadness in his voice. *"You cannot fight fate"*, consoled Ganapathi. Michael nodded in return and they went back to the dance floor.

The dance stopped promptly at 10.30 pm. Some of the ex-students went to sleep. Some sat down and had a drink. Manoj Suri carried a bar in his boxes and served drinks to all who asked. Another group of ex-students started playing cards.

Some of the girls had come into the boys' dormitory

and soon an impromptu Antakshri started with two groups choosing themselves. Usha Nair was the star singer on one side. The number of songs that she knew and remembered were amazing. She was ably assisted by the extremely charming and pretty, Ruksana Lakdawalla, who was an air hostess.

On the other side, Ganapathi sang such old songs that many of the juniors did not know at all. They wondered if they were actually songs or if he was making them up extempore. They believed he was quite capable of making them up. At the end of the singing session, the younger boys started calling him Guru Antakshri. He assured them that all the songs he had sung were real ones, sung by a late legendary singer, Mukesh, who was Neil Nitin Mukesh's grandfather.

The drinkers called it a day at 1 am, while the gamblers stayed awake till 4 am.

On the next day, a few more Alumni members came. The 1969 head boy, Dilip Rao, was there, as also Harbhajan Singh Dhupar, who had lost a lot of weight since his school days. The mischievous Khusru Irani was also there, with his dapper cap. He was a successful electrician in the Middle East now. His country cousins, Nalini and Usha, had also come and it was a happy reunion. Vishaka Sarnajame, whom Ganapathi called Indira Gandhi, because of her nose, was also there.

Reunion Sports Contests

On this day, the cricket match was between the Alumni and the staff. The Principal, Julian Luke, was also playing. He was a very good bowler and also very sporting. It was supposed to be a 20 over match. Half way through the match, the ex-students realized that they had a very low score, so they wanted to change it to a 25 over match. The Principal agreed, as it did not make much of a difference.

Ganapathi, as usual, was one of the commentators. The Principal was seated to his left, and his friends were in the audience. The staff was now batting second.

Ganapathi commented, *"The staff look like they are going to overhaul the alumni total easily and the alumni have no answers to Thakoor's lusty hitting. We have two very rich businessmen here - Manoj Suri, who makes Table Tennis tables, has decided to donate one table to the school; and Barinder Katyal, who is a distributor for Hero Motorcorps, has decided to donate one Hero bike to the Principal".* Both the friends started laughing along with the Principal. He continued, *"On my right is our Principal, and on his right are two fat men. The grey haired fellow is Manoj Suri and the black haired fellow is Barinder Katyal. Please give them a big hand for their generosity."*

The students clapped loudly and turned around to look at the embarrassed pair.

Ganapathi continued, *"Barinder Katyal was my*

classmate; how come his hair is still black? Archie Pitchiyani, please do not block my vision, you are not transparent. Marissa, you are wearing a lovely superman top. (Marissa a 9th standard student was his friend Adi Soonawalla's child.) *Thakoor hits another boundary and the alumni total looks totally inadequate".*

Munnu relieved him and took over the commentary. Ganapathi went and sat with Suri and Katyal. A student interviewed Suri about his tenure at Barnes and his Table Tennis business for the *Barnicle*. She was happy with his answers and went away happy. *"You are a celebrity, Suri",* said Nadar. *"Thanks to your big mouth",* Suri replied.

Shapoor Izadiyar was the one who batted for long. He is the cricketing coach of the Iran national team. At the other end, the ex-students kept getting out. Christopher Phillips hit a mighty six, but did not stick around for long. The Alumni lost this match too.

In the Alumni football team, there were lots of youngsters, led by Julian Luke, the Principal's son. They beat the current students. Also, there was a match in the swimming pool. The same set of youngsters beat the current students. Thus, the Alumni's cricket misery was forgotten.

Famous Alumni

Kaisar Dupaishi had also come for the reunion, but he did not stay at Barnes. He was now the Principal of an international school. He preferred to stay on a farm in Devlali, which belonged to one of his students from Barnes. Kaisar had been a teacher at Barnes too. He was married to a Barnes' teacher and they had a lovely daughter.

Ruallah Naimi spent most of his time clicking pictures and some of them were really lovely. Denise Tully also carried a camera, but she clicked only with the students. Later, she uploaded the pictures on the Facebook for those students who had not been able to come for the reunion. She was very popular with the students.

Talat Jani was another very entertaining ex-student. He was a movie director and always had plenty of stories at his beck and call to tell.

The surprise Alumni this year was Arshad Warsi, a big star in Bollywood. He was a very good sport. He posed for selfies with every Alumni and the current students, and the staff. His ready smile never left his face. He was truly happy to be back in Barnes where he had studied all those years in the past. His brother, Iqbal Warsi, also from Barnes, had also come. Arshad stayed in the Principal's guest room, but he spent the whole day with his friends.

Jeetu Ahuja was built like Sylvestor Stallone. He chatted with Talat Jani and Vicky Gurnani. *"Hero, Director and Villain"*, remarked Ganapathi. *"Why, me a villain?"* Vicky asked. *"You remind me of Kader Khan"* was the ready reply.

Felicitating Teachers

Kaisar Dupaishi was the Chairman of the Alumni Association. Before the dance that night, there was a ceremony to honour the teachers.

Mr Gadre, who was invited and honored, gave a heart touching speech, where most of the Alumni had tears in their eyes. The other teacher honored was Mr Thorpe. Among the present teachers, they gave awards to two teachers who produced the best ISC results. Kaisar gave a nice speech too. Ganapathi later grumbled to him that he too deserved a prize for his running commentary during all those reunion games. Kaisar Dupaishi promised him one the next year.

There were drinks for those interested. Soon all the teachers left and only the students were there. One of the ex-students got drunk and caused a ruckus. He was banned from all future reunions. There was another young ex-student, who stole cigarettes and drinks from the other ex-students and distributed them to the current students. He too was banned for all future reunions.

On the next day, some of the students left after breakfast and the rest left after lunch.

The 2014 & 2016 Reunions

The 2014 Reunion

THE 2014 reunion was more fun than the previous year, as now they knew many more students from across the ages. Earlier, they knew only those who had been students at Barnes during their own time. The youngest students that they became friends with were from the batch of 2010.

Ganapathi adopted Hemalatha Choudhary, who was a wisp of a girl. He spent a lot of time trying to make her eat more. She was in her final year B.Com, but still looked like a school girl. Minal Jadhav was extremely pretty and also a college student in Kalyan. Their classmate, Afreen Khan, worked in Mumbai, as she had found a good job. Another girl from their time, Renu Gurung, also worked in Mumbai. That they had become friends with Barnicles of the Seventies speaks volumes about the Barnes spirit.

Lateef was another ex-student, who built a tennis court, with lights, for the school. The Alumni had made cash donations for this. Colin Massey collected money for a water cooler and had it installed in the dining hall. The Alumni always tried to do something for their old school in their own individual ways.

On the morning of their departure, there were games and prizes for the Prep house kids for which the Alumni had donated 500 rupees each. The children were happy.

Kaisar Hakeem had promised Ganapathi a lift to Nasik. He and Hemu went with him. They stopped at a mall to have some snacks and chatted for a while. Then, he dropped her at her hostel and waited at the nearby road crossing. This was the corner where the road that came from Devlali joined the Mumbai-Nasik highway.

His friend, Adi Soonawalla, had come to the school with his wife to take his daughter, Marissa, out for the weekend. They had dropped her back at the school and were now on their way to Mumbai. They picked up Ganapathi on the way.

"Podgy, when we met in Barnes in 1978, did you ever think that 40 years later, your daughter would be studying in my school and you would be giving me a lift to Mumbai?" Ganapathi reflected. *"Never even imagined it"*, said Adi

Soonawalla, as he drove at a comfortable speed.

They stopped for tea and snacks, and a cigarette, on their way, on the highway. Once they entered Mumbai, the traffic increased multifold. Ganapathi got off at Vikhroli, where Adi turned into the Andheri road. He caught a rickshaw to Sion. On the way, he stopped at Godrej Colony, in Vikhroli, to meet his Mumbai adopted daughter, Pooja Mishra. He had bought her raisins from Nasik, which is a grapes growing area. He did not want to carry it with him. She came down to take it. He gave her a big hug and left for his hotel.

The 2016 Reunion

The reunion in 2016 was the most crowded, as more than a 100 students turned up. Facebook had really made the reunion popular.

As usual, Ganapathi arrived on a Thursday and, as usual, Munnu was already there before him. Munnu's son was also an ex-student of Barnes and now he was a teacher there. He was also a very good sportsman.

Rustom, as usual, arrived late in the night. *"Shapoor came from Iran just for this but could not make it, as he has fallen ill in Mumbai"* he reported.

Kaisar Hakeem arrived on Saturday, as his work kept him busy on Thursday and Friday. *"This year, I could make it only for a day, I tried calling Masud Alam Khan but, as usual, he refused, citing some excuse"*, he told his friends.

The younger lot of girls also arrived, but only for a day. Hemlatha, Minal and Afreen came and hugged Ganapathi hard. He was very fond of them and always kept in touch.

Renu arrived on Sunday when it was time to leave. *"I did not come for the reunion, as I have a new job and can't take leave. I came to meet you all and Mam, she is unwell in Devlali"* she explained.

Munnu Hussain was the senior most, as he had left Barnes in 1960. For the last two years, Rudy became the senior most at the reunion. He had graduated in 1955. He had come with the elegant Pam, who was delightful.

Kaisar Hakeem gave Ganapathi a lift, as usual, to Nasik. The young girls also squeezed in. Five people huddled together on the back seat. As this was Barnes, they managed. At Devlali, Hemu, Afreen and Renu disembarked to meet a retired Barnes' teacher who was unwell. Minal and Ganapathi carried on to Nasik with Kaisar. He dropped them off at the Nasik-Mumbai cab service.

Ganapathi hired a cab to Mumbai and dropped Minal on the way.

When they left Barnes all those years ago, they had thought that a part of their life was over. It really wasn't. The reunions helped them keep that memory alive and, for three days in the year, they rejoiced in their childhood again.

Prem Verma, who organized the reunions, always sent

an invite, which read–*"Thursday, the time to arrive and meet old friends. Sunday, the time to say your good byes and start counting the days to the next reunion."* A far cry from the time we were in the school and counted the days to go home.

It is true we attend one reunion and the rest of the year count the days to the next reunion and wonder when we can be back to the place that has so many childhood memories, so much laughter and so much fun, our heaven on the earth–The School on the Hill!

Memories of Barnes

IT HAS been 43 years since I graduated from Barnes and still some memories come flashing by. I used to dream about Barnes when I was at college but now the dreams have stopped. I think of my day-scholar classmates - Jyoti Walke, Sudipta Choudhury, Madhavai Abhyankar (she had blue eyes), Ambika Talwar, Cyrus Irani, Raj Unny, Dhirendra Nehra, whose lunch we used to rob regularly.

The boys that we used to give money to go to the Tuck shop, after finishing their lunch, and the girls we never bothered about. I think the boarder girls used to feed them when we nasties relieved them of their food.

I remember Satish Pardeshi, the smallest boy in our dormitory, and Ali Razvi, the smallest boy in our class.

Ali, despite his size, was very mischievous. I remember my cousin, Rajalakshmi, and her husband, Loganathan, had come to see me. Mr Davis told them, *"Don't kidnap him"*. Then he smiled. I was too surprised to reply.

I remember the lovely snacks the Middle Eastern students would bring with them. I remember my junior, Barkat Pirani, who had such a warm smile. His elder brother, Ismail, was a businessman even when he was at the school.

I often think of Mr Hoffman, and his inspections on Sundays when we had to blanco our keds and polish our shoes. Hoffy used to actually peep into our ears to check if we had washed them and also smell our socks to make sure they have been washed. Imagine smelling 120 pairs of socks. He was one diligent house master.

Hoffy's Scout uniform was also a delight. He used to wear these enormous half pants and stockings that almost reached the pant helm. He also used to cycle at the same speed for miles together. Never fast and never slow.

Whenever we went to Hoffy to complain that someone was bullying us, he had this gentle advice, *"You must not tell me this, you must go to your prefect. If I have to deal with these matters, they will call you a snitch for telling teachers what happens in the dorm. That is unpardonable in Boarding School. Tell your prefect and they will take the action. That is why they are there."*

Mr Russel, our Mathematics teacher, was 6 feet 7 inches

tall. He used to drown his hair in oil and plaster it tight over his head. This led to his pet name, *Chapiya*.

Mr Mainguy was very strong physically and his biceps were the biggest in the school. He was innocent where guile was concerned. When he was the MOD, students could get away with bizaree excuses for being late. Always wondered if he knew we were lying or was he just innocent. He had a nasal voice, so the boys called him *Tatturi*.

Mr Mainguy's sister was our Mum Peron. She was the sweetest and best mum we ever had. She really loved her brother, Mainguy, and spoke about him all the time.

Mr Gupta, our Hindi teacher, always chewed *supari* and had a habit of speaking from one side of his mouth. The boys used to have fun imitating the way he spoke. He really had a beautiful wife, who was not a teacher.

Mr Bhalerao, our Marathi teacher, had a moustache like the smuggler Haji Mastaan. His motto was, *"Always keep both ends polished and shining"*. True to this, his shoes were always shining and his hair was also shining, precisely combed with oil, and glowing.

Mr Swing was a favourite with the students with his stories about outer space and other small gems of knowledge. He was also our house mentor and coached us when we had debates and elocution. When he spoke, it was not his mouth only, his eyes, his hands and his entire body spoke to us. He was very expressive.

Mr Donald Alfred Smith would give Donald Trump a run for his money. He was one of the most jovial English teachers, who would keep talking about Mrs Smith on her way to him on a truck. However, when he got angry, he would shake and blow up like a volcano. At that time, his face would become completely red and his voice would sound like a thunder breaking on our head. He was a gem of a teacher. Once, in Elocution final, when I had to say, *"If Music be the food of love, play on"*, he actually hid behind the curtains and whistled till I said, *"Enough! No more! It's not as sweet now as it was before"*.

Mr Davis, who would go for long walks, from his office to Candy block, mostly smiled at the students who wished him. Sometimes, he used to crack jokes and they were extremely witty. He never took classes, but he was a very good teacher. Once, he came in to replace *Chapiya*, who was unwell that day. I still remember the way he taught us the Pythagoras theorem. Others said it sounded better because they had paid a close attention to him, being the Principal. Our regular Mathematics teacher never received that kind of attention.

I remember the athletics finals, where Debra Dameron used to come first in every race, followed by the Phillips twins, Rosemary and Rosellin. Sometimes, the teachers were confused which twin came second and which third.

The swimming pools were our favourite haunt in

summer. We used to sneak off for a swim whenever we got the opportunity. The MOD usually ignored this if a senior was with us. If juniors went by themselves, if caught, three of the best was a minimum of caning.

Our Vice-Principal, Mr Roberts, did look like one of the Kennedys, and he had such a booming voice. He did not use loud speakers. He was a very handsome man, and also very interested in sports. He encouraged the boys on the field.

The thin Sister Misquita who was in-charge of the hospital, could comfort a sick child and, at the same time, take a faker to task. She had two very well-built boys, who looked nothing like her thin self. They were very sweet boys. Cyril was one of them, who saved Surjit Singh Kheer who had dived into the diving pool without knowing how to swim.

I relive the memories of Rosemary tying me a rakhee 48 years ago and the 17 rakhees I had in my final year at Barnes. I often think of my first crush at 13 with a smile, as she was not only very pretty but extremely thoughtful and sweet. She had a temper though.

My first head boy and house captain, Dilip Rao, winning the 1,500 m finals, with Douglas Kerr breathing down his neck, was a sight to behold. Michael Scott whizzing down the track and smiling at the same time was another beautiful memory.

In cricket, hitting the only four in my life at Barnes, in

the B team, is another memory that I will cherish. It was a square cut and the students had cheered. They could not believe that I could hit a boundary. I was sent in to bat at number 11 after the bowlers, as I was the worst player in the team.

I cannot still forget the 200 m race in swimming, where I finished 15 minutes after the last boy before me. They waited for me to finish the race and the students wanted me to get a finishing certificate. Mr Davis shot the idea down.

In 10th standard, we actually had a gang of Asif Velani, Ravinandan and myself for the sole purpose of relieving day-scholar Raj Unny of his lunch. Raj was a good sport and happily ate at the canteen. Floyd Vaz was another day-scholar, who could argue for hours. He was one determined boy who Mohanty was very fond of.

Bernadette Brown, Margaret Keenan, Bernadette Vinden, Jennifer Dameron, the blonde Gloria Smith, the gorgeous Lorraine Canthem and Lorraine Ryder, the smart Lorraine Rose, and the highly popular Colleen Edge - who can forget these unmatched beauties? For elegance, there was Erica D'Abreo and, a decade later, her cute little sister, Fiona. All of them had their own fan clubs at the school. Anna Young and Linda Middlecoat were the cute ones and my classmate, Madhavi Abhyankar, had amazing blue eyes.

In the swimming pool, one had to watch Glenn Arnold against the Khambatta brothers to know what speed was.

One had to see Rustom Parvaresh swimming with the twins, Sharukh and Jimmy, to know what family genes meant in sports.

In Boxing, Crighton Watts, Noel Edge, Clyde Arnold, Christopher and Keith Phillips, Michael Bardey, and Valentine Edge were a critic's delight.

Mr Gama's colourful language, when you did something the wrong way on the field, was amusing and, at the same time, he got the message across. You bloody well buck up!

In boxing, Mr Mainguy's short left jab, which could knock you out for the better part of the hour, and Mr Gama's impenetrable defence would stand us in good stead in the later part of life when we came up against bullies.

Miss D'sa telling us how to pronounce a word will remain forever etched in my brain. She could give you a cold stare for wrong usage of a word, which you could carry to your grave. She was very fond of Margaret Andrews. Bossie Maggie spoke impeccable English and she was the only one I know who would correct your grammar in spoken English.

The singers, Jennifer Dameron, Lorna Massey and Caroline Mannings could hold the entire school spellbound when they sang. Evans Hall would be filled with their voice and the applause would always be deafening.

Mr Coles retired in 1968, but he did come back for two events in 1969. The three cheers that the boys gave him were so loud that it looked the stone buildings were vibrating because of resonance. He was a much loved soul.

The attendants in the mess we used to bribe for the best mutton pieces at night. The *hamal* in the dormitory who used to buy us *bidis* and also bet for us at the *matka* in bagur.

The two Tuck shop men will remain in our hearts till we pass away. What goodies! They used to give us food on credit if they thought we were hungry. They could not see a hungry student and do nothing about it. They had to fill our stomachs and we were hungry all the time. Bada Sayi could also put you in your place if you pushed a boy ahead in line very strongly and very firmly. You dare not misbehave in his Tuck shop.

A hockey ball, sailing fast and high through the air, and Shahab Fikri jutting out his chest to stop it, has been a most unforgettable and a never-to-be-repeated feat. As also Harbhajan Singh Dhupar standing in front of the hockey goal and there was no goal visible.

A student called Daddy by the entire school, including teachers, was Mosadique Haghighi. His girlfriend was the prettiest girl in the school. When they danced together, it was like a Barbie Doll dancing with Goliath.

Once in the morning assembly, we were singing hymns. Suddenly, the music stopped and C Paul at the piano got up and screamed, *"Is this the way to sing a hymn; all of you are out of sync?"* The whole school was shocked, but the ultimate reminder came from Principal Davis, *"I agree that the singing is atrocious by all standards, but no member of the staff should get excited when I am here".*

Richard White being chased all over the field by Mr Mainguy; Mr Walsh falling on his face, with his hands to protect him; and Parvez Razvi doing gymnastics have been the images that have stayed with us over the ages.

Then we had these boys, with unbelievable stamina, who could run for hours - Dilip Rao, Gangadhar Jadhav, Surjit Singh Kheer and Sharukh Yazdagardi.

The speedsters - Douglas Kerr, Michael Scott and Christopher Phillips will always be remembered. Debra Dameron, among girls, used to float on the field as she was so thin.

The cooks at Barnes, who used to boil everything, and the two boys in Prep house, who robbed the Tuck shop regularly, with the help of a hockey stick and a fishing net, will always be remembered. They used to knock the food into the net and bring it out. It took the staff more than a month to figure out the modus operandi. And the boys were still in Prep house, meaning they were under ten and had already figured out the ingenuous idea.

The quaint post office, which was barely a 50 square feet area under the stair case of Evans Hall and yet boasted of its own pin code!

The flag post to which we had to run to if we were late for a meal. Blind well to run round and round; and the quarries to smoke and swim will remain forever etched in our young minds.

Mr Gadre's acerbic wit; Mr Hoffman's numbering all orders; and Mr Smith acting out a part in literature, cannot be matched in any school in the world.

The keenly contested sports and the fiercely contested debates made us what we are today; ready to compete with the best in the world. And the idea of fairness in all that we do was the *mantra* of every teacher at Barnes. They made it clear that liars and cheats had no place at Barnes.

The camaraderie of the borders, and the love that we shared with each other, could be seen in the tears when we parted and the bear hugs when we meet years later all over the world. Do you know a Barnes' get together in the United States had 75 people attending?

Now, there is a reunion at Barnes that attracts over a 100 students and one in Pune that attracts over 150 people. The strings of love never ending, boarding school bonds are something else.

The pillars of Barnes are not the ones at Evans Hall, but the teachers - Mr S B Gadre, Mr Gama, Mr Walsh, Mr D V Hoffman, Miss D'sa, Mr C Paul, Mr Thorpe, Mr Mishra, Mr Davis, Mrs Michael, Mr Michael, Mr Smith, Mr Russel, Mr Mainguy and Mum Peron.

Who can forget the shrill voice of Mum Tully, piercing the mist at 6 am in the morning, and her steady music on every bed rail with the singing words, "Wake up boys, wake up"? Not that it had much effect, but it was the start of a winter day when we lazed happily under our blankets.

The bunking school and going to Devlali to eat or for a movie. The raiding of guava and grape farms; the swim in Dharna river, where a student almost drowned during a scout outing, and I dived in to save him and almost drowned myself. Riyaz Hussain saved both of us and then screamed at me for trying to save the other boy. *"Do you know how to save a drowning boy? You don't; you can't swim to save your own life. So why the hell did you jump in, you misfit idiot black man?"* He was really angry. Mr Lois, the junior Scout Master, was equally angry, but happy that all had ended well and everyone was alive. He was the one responsible for the boys' safety.

The market permits, which were used only for eating. Visiting the small, but incredibly delicious, Maulana and Mathura Dairy Farm for endless number of sweets stayed long after school. I looked for both when I went back after 39 years; but I could not find them. The day permits, that we would use for watching two movies, and then how ten boys would squeeze into one cab to get back to the school on time.

She gave me a rose one day. I kept that rose in my book within its pages for a year after that. The notes that we ·····ed to the ones we loved. The silly sorrow when you could not catch her eye in the dining hall though you sat more than 100 feet away.

Brother's Hour, where you had a line of couples standing under trees, and among a dozen couples there was only one couple who were actually siblings. Ravinandan Mohanty had a sister, Bina, in the school. He was always playing during Brother's Hour. Ask about his sister and he would say, "What is there to talk to her?" Even when she approached him, it was always a one sentence reply. But, as she was younger to him, she never let this bother her.

Both sets of twins, Jimmy and Sharukh, and Rosemary and Roselin, were extremely good at sports, but not so smart in the classroom.

Mr C Paul's younger brother, R Paul, later joined as a music teacher. He was extremely talented and a bachelor. The boys used to pair him, in their mind, with various unmarried teachers, but nothing like that ever happened.

The Principal's son, Michael Davis, won every elocution and debate that he participated in. He was good, but students never gave him credit for that. They thought he won because he was the Princy's son.

The outings with the Scouts were always fun. Going to Devlali by bus and then hiring cycles. We saw the entire country side in this manner. And the food packed by the mess staff would actually be tasty when we ate it outdoors.

Falling in love and falling out of love was a regular affair those days. Wearing a ring which had her initials was the trend.

The Sunday white clothes that we had starched was the only day we actually stayed clean. Otherwise, dirt and the Barnicle were first cousins.

The smoke that came out of our mouths on winter mornings! The sweaters and blazers that we wore had the same colours.

The counting of days to go back home! Holidays meant we saw 45 movies in 30 days. Still puzzled about how we could manage that.

The helplessness that we felt when, at the end of cross-country run, we had to run up from Gate Lodge at a time when we could not even walk. But we ran! Yes, we did and that made us what we are today. A Barnicle never gives up.

***